UNCHIPPED: LUNA

UNCHIPPED: LUNA

TAYA DEVERE

DVM PRESS

DVM Press
Vaakunatie 16 D 14
20780 Kaarina, Suomi-Finland
www.dvmpress.com
www.tayadevere.com

ISBN 978-952-7404-11-9 First Ebook Edition
ISBN 978-952-7404-12-6 First Print Edition

Cover Design © 2020 by Deranged Doctor Design - www.derangeddoctordesign.com
Ebook formatting by Polgarus Studios – www.polgarusstudios.com
Editing by Christopher Scott Thompson and Lindsay Fara Kaplan

To all underdogs out there:
The black sheep, the odd ducks, the rejects, the loners.
You make this world go around.

A SOLDIER'S MIND

A short story in the world of the Unchipped series

The helmet falls on the dirt floor. Three men pass Jovan without stopping to pick it up. They don't look back either, to tell him they're sorry for knocking it down.

Because they aren't.

Bumping into Jovan's rolling tool chest was anything but unintentional. He wets his lips and takes another bite of his sliced soy-based ham and cream cheese sandwich.

A pair of steel-toed boots stops next to the fallen hardhat. "Hey, egghead. Mind if I join you?"

Jovan looks up and smiles at Dunja. After he nods, his coworker joins him on a bench made of two wooden blocks and a wide board. The board wobbles as Dunja finds a comfortable seat. Then she digs into her lunch box.

"Minnie Mouse?" Jovan says, eyeing the blue metal lunchbox with the famous critter printed on its side. Dunja shrugs, picking out a can of vegetable soup, a flask and a pack of cigarettes.

"Better her than whatever the fuck the kids look up to these days."

"It figures that you're a Minnie supporter."

Dunja works the can open and tosses the lid on the ground. "What?" She takes a long sip of soup. She chews on the cold potatoes and carrots.

"I bet Mickey didn't stand a chance."

Dunja rolls her eyes, but Jovan sees the side of her mouth twitching. "Look at you," she says, swallowing the cold soup. "Turning ancient cartoon characters into a battle of the sexes."

Jovan takes a bite of his sandwich. The sunlight reflects off a pallet of tiles. They laid half of the building's first floor yesterday. Today, they'll stay as long as it takes to get the rest of it done.

His mouth full, Jovan mumbles, "Go ahead. Admit it. You didn't even glance in Mickey's direction."

Dunja chuckles and takes another swig of soup. "What? Just because I'm gay, I can't have a thing for strong, cheerful men like Mickey? Maybe Minnie was all that was available. Did you ever think of that, egghead?"

Jovan nods at the Minnie Mouse lunch box and raises his eyebrows. "Well, was she?"

Dunja scoffs. "Whatever, man. Since when has Micky Mouse been a phallic symbol anyway?"

"Oh wow, we're talking *dicks* now? Do you really want to go there?"

"You started it, man."

They sit and eat in comfortable silence. A buzzer goes off by the construction site offices—all five of which are made of shipping containers—prompting Jovan and Dunja to get up from their wobbly seat.

"Hey, did you get signed up for that chipping interview thingy?" she asks.

Jovan picks up his hardhat, puts it back on. "I thought the *thingy* was basically mandatory." He smirks at Dunja's poor vocabulary.

"Fuck off, Einstein. Did you, or did you not?"

Jovan waves her off. "I will," he says. "Just need more information first. Did you see their latest brochure? Thing couldn't be more vague if they tried."

"Yeah, I saw it. It is what it is. But what more information do you need?" Dunja asks. "Like you said, it's mandatory."

"Basically mandatory. If you want to keep your job."

The three men return to their workspace. The one who bumped into Jovan's toolbox—Filip—stomps over. He nods at Jovan's tools, spread on a full piece of plywood. "Borrow your tapping block?"

Dunja wipes her hands on the front of her pants and nods at Jovan to tell him she's returning to her own workstation. Jovan smiles at her and then turns to look at Filip. "I'd prefer you didn't."

"Huh?"

"The last time you borrowed a tool of mine, you returned it covered in blood."

"The nail gun? I told you there was an accident," Filip says, waving him off. "They're tools. Shit gets dirty."

"Sure. I just prefer it's *my* excrement and bodily fluids on *my* things. Not yours."

"Your *what* now?"

Jovan sighs and turns his back on Filip. "Shit and blood. I got plenty of my own, so I have no need for yours." Jovan picks up his work gloves and starts to pull them on. "Just take the damn block. If it's not too much trouble, just wipe it after with—"

Two hands shove Jovan from the back. He stumbles forward and catches himself on the plywood table. After finding his feet, he turns around. "Listen, Filip, I don't want any prob—"

Filip's fist lands on the side of Jovan's nose. He flies backward and crashes down where his hardhat had landed earlier.

"Piece of shit…" Filip mumbles. He grabs the tapping block and stomps away.

Jovan sits up. He wipes his face, leaving a smear of blood on his glove. "Great… just…" He tries to stand up, but he's too dizzy from the blow.

In the distance, Dunja turns and spots Jovan on the ground. She starts jogging toward him. Jovan waves her off, not wanting her to bother. "I'm okay…" he murmurs. Supporting his weight on his hands, Jovan tries to get up but falls back down into the dirt. The world spins.

Dunja extends her hand to him. "What the hell happened?" Jovan lets the woman help him up.

"Just a misunderstanding."

"With Filip?"

"Yeah. Apparently, the word *excrement* is too defamatory to be used around here."

"Shit, man."

"Exactly."

"Tell me you didn't correct that asshole's vocabulary?"

"Can't correct something that isn't there."

Dunja wipes shavings and dirt off of Jovan's coveralls.

"You can't go around educating people, egghead." She lets go of Jovan and pushes her hardhat back on her head. Her thick, night-black hair pushes back against it, leaving the helmet floating too high.

"I just don't want him taking my stuff, is all."

"Just deal with it. Filip is a hemorrhoid—a pain in the ass that won't go away. Everybody knows it. And everybody tolerates his fuckery day in day out."

"But it's not right. Who is he to treat people like dirt?"

Dunja sighs. From her chest pocket, she pulls out a flask and offers it to Jovan. He rolls the cap open and takes a sip. The pungent taste of *rakija* fills his mouth and burns his throat. Dunja shakes her head slowly, watching Jovan take a big gulp of the liquor she carries around in a flask. Why—Jovan doesn't know. He's never seen Dunja drunk. Not even tipsy. Maybe she brings it with her for emergencies like these.

"Give me that..." she says, taking the flask from Jovan. After shoving it back in her chest pocket, Dunja nudges him on the shoulder.

"Next time that fuck-face comes around, just think: would you rather be right, or would you rather stay alive?"

Jovan is relieved that his head is clear now. After taking that punch from Filip, he'd been worried that he might have a concussion. He steers the motorcycle, zigzagging between self-driving and electric cars. The cars all drive with a galling lack of speed toward downtown Belgrade. The bike's manual control is on—Jovan prefers his bike not to have a will of its own. Self-driving vehicles freak him out, though the city hasn't had a traffic accident for almost six months.

The wind humming outside his helmet, Jovan makes his way into the heart of the city. Belgrade. Or the City of Serbia, as people have started to call it as of late. Too many things are changing, too much information locked inside the ChipNet, which Jovan would rather not use. But the information the local newspapers and television give him is limited these days. All foreign broadcasts have been canceled. The TV now has only four channels to choose from; Wellness-Channel, Happiness-Channel, AR-store, Chip-Info.

Jovan needs to know what he's signing up for. If he's signing up for anything.

On the ground outside the Chip-Center, Jovan sees the same tiles he's been installing at the job site for weeks now. He walks through a revolving door and enters the humming building. The busy lobby space and the corridor beyond are filled with people trying on AR-glasses and walking around, nodding at each other, smiling.

"Can I help you, sir?"

Jovan spins around and stares at a man dressed in purple overalls and a genuine-seeming smile.

"Yes." He clears his throat, suddenly nervous but having no idea why. "I have questions about the chipping and the Happiness-Program," Jovan says. "Whom should I talk to?"

"We're delighted to hear that you're so eager to get started with the program, sir. Are you currently employed by the city?"

"Yes. I work at the construction site on the harbor side of the city. Project Nursery."

"Just one moment, sir." The purple man puts on a set of AR-glasses and starts tapping and sweeping the air. After a minute or two, he takes off the glasses and smiles at Jovan. "Great news, sir. Your job site is scheduled for chipping interviews as early as tomorrow morning. All your questions will be answered during a face-to-face meeting with one of our experts."

"That's..." He's unsure what to say. "Can't I just talk to someone here? Someone who's in charge of technology and science?"

"Sir?"

"The brain implants. I have questions."

The purple man tilts his head. A confused smile Jovan supposes is apologetic spreads across his face. "Unfortunately, the head of the program is unavailable at the moment. But I can assure you the specialists sent to your place of work will have all the answers you need."

"But that's not—"

"You will have to excuse me, sir. There are others waiting in line."

Jovan looks over his shoulder. A few people with AR-glasses wander aimlessly nearby, but no one is waiting in line behind him. "There's no one here."

The purple man smiles and points at his AR-glasses. Then he waves Jovan goodbye.

Outside, the open, brightly tiled yard is mostly empty. Only two men and two women, all wearing urban style camo coveralls, sit by the water fountain. They pass a vape around and talk with low voices. Jovan's about to put on his helmet and jump on his bike. Changing his mind, he shoves the helmet under his arm and walks over. He raises his hand in a hello.

"Hey guys. Can I bum a puff or two?"

The woman holding the vape looks Jovan over from head to toe. "Sure thing, hon." She takes a step closer and winks at him. "You here to pick up your gear?"

"My what?"

The other woman reaches for the vape pen and takes it before Jovan has a chance to grab it. "Vesna, we're not supposed to talk to them before they're recruited."

But Vesna doesn't seem to listen to her friend. She nods at Jovan's motorcycle, waiting next to the Chip-Center's revolving door. "How fast does that thing go?"

"How do you know it's mine?"

The group chuckles. They exchange amused looks. One of the men gestures for Vesna to come back and join their circle. "Leave the poor guy alone, Vesna. I'm sure he has enough problems without you harassing him."

"Harassing, my ass..." Vesna says but steps backward and joins her colleagues by the fountain. "Drive safe, biker-boy."

Jovan returns to his bike and is about to put on his helmet when a hand touches his shoulder. The fourth man hands over the vape. He hasn't said anything up until now. His coworkers walk back into the building. "Sorry about that, bud," he says to Jovan. "They get cocky so freaking fast. Now that they feel important for the first time in their lives."

Jovan takes the vape and frowns. "Important? Why?" He takes a puff, then another.

"They're soldiers now. Chipped soldiers. It gives them a sense of power and entitlement."

Jovan hands the vape pen back to the soldier. His white and gray attire looks like it's never been worn before, the fabric crisp and new. "But not you?"

The man shrugs. He takes a puff, and puts the vape into his chest pocket. "It's irrelevant, what I feel. All I know is I don't want to end up downstairs. Being a soldier is just one way to avoid it."

"Avoid—what?"

"Getting plugged in."

"Who's plugged in? What do you mean?"

"Can't really confirm much. What I do know is that not all people are suitable for working and living in the new city. They pick and choose."

"By what terms?"

"By what you're worth. To them. As a human being."

Jovan holds his breath. An uneasy feeling takes him over. "And those they consider worthless??"

The soldier shrugs and turns to leave. "That's above my pay grade," he says. "All I know is that they limit the number of people moving in. Something about city resources."

"Limit how?"

"Like I said, I don't know the specifics. And I'd rather keep it that way too."

"You don't want to know?" Jovan shakes his head in disbelief. "Why the hell wouldn't you want to know?"

The soldier gives him a small smile. "Because I couldn't bear to be the one who decides who's valuable and who gets shut down like last year's smartphone."

The car has followed him the whole way from the Chip-Center to his front yard. Jovan takes his helmet off, staring at the vehicle's tinted windows. He sidesteps away from his bike and spreads his hands to whoever sits inside. Maybe he should be scared. Maybe he should run upstairs to his apartment and lock the door. Something. But the annoyance of first having information withheld from him and then being spied on comes out as uncharacteristic aggression.

What would Filip do, he finds himself thinking, and he doesn't like this hostile thought one bit.

The car's passenger side door opens. A well-groomed, fifty-something man wearing green-blinking AR-glasses walks out. Calm and collected, he takes a step toward Jovan, then stops and turns around. He takes off the glasses and tosses them into his car. Relaxed and steady footsteps bring him over.

"Why the hell are you following me?" Jovan asks, his voice ruder than he's ever heard it before. He really needs to get some rest. But the way the adrenaline now rushes through him, he already knows it'll be a sleepless night.

"Apologies, my young friend." The sharp-faced man extends his hand, his dark eyes cooly assessing Jovan. "The name is Ef." Jovan hesitates but shakes Ef's hand anyway. "I hated to tail you like that, but I couldn't help but overhear your inquiries back at the Chip-Center and I hoped we could talk."

So he's not only following Jovan, but he's also eavesdropping?

"Okay. And?"

"And I may have some answers for you."

"May?"

"Well, it depends on your questions entirely. If you are driving around the city, trying to find out what the meaning of life is, there's not much I can do for you. But if you'd like to learn more about the chipping and how the city truly operates, I can help."

Jovan stares at the man, who smiles and holds his gaze, patiently waiting for Jovan to make up his mind. Something is different about him, but not in a bad way. Jovan can't quite put his finger on it. He folds his arms and nods at Ef's vehicle, the sliding door still open.

"Your glasses."

"What about them?"

"They have a green light."

"They do."

"Why is that? I've only ever seen purple ones."

"Every AR-city has its own color. Where I'm from, it's green."

"And where are you from?"

"Doesn't matter. That's not why I'm here."

"Matters to me."

"I'm from the green city. City of California. But that's not the question you should be asking. Not how this conversation is supposed to go." The man smiles when Jovan gestures to him to elaborate. "Here's what I'd like to know myself. Why are you so interested to hear about chipping technology?"

Jovan stares at the man without answering. He's Chipped, no doubt, and from what he can tell someone of importance. It's the way he carries himself, the way he talks. But then again, something's different. Something in his eyes that most ChipReps lack.

Kindness.

Jovan clears his throat. "I need to know what I'm agreeing to, before I go through this process. *If* I go through it. And something tells me that these job site interviews are more like sales pitches than scientific explanations."

A brief laugh. An approving nod. "You've got that right."

"So, you know how the chip works? What they can and can't do with it? You know what that guy meant when he said he didn't want to be plugged in?"

"I do know."

"Which part?"

"All of it."

"How?"

"Well… Have you ever heard of an organization called CFU?"

Jovan wets his lips. For some reason, his heart has started to race against his chest.

"I thought organizations of any sort were a thing of past?"

"So you haven't heard of us?"

Jovan waves him off. "You know what, I'm not in

the mood for playing games. And I'm not looking to join some green city cult, either." He turns to leave, but hesitates. This man might be his only chance to learn about what's to come.

"Hey, whoa." Jovan turns back and sees the man raise his palms in the air. "I'm not here to recruit you, if that's what you're worried about."

"What then?"

"I'm here to give you answers. Plain and simple. So you can ask your questions and hear my answers. Then, if you're interested, I'll tell you more about CFU."

He's telling the truth, Jovan can tell. Or Ef's the best liar he's ever met. Jovan looks around the yard, then up to the balconies. Three or more heads pull back in when his nosey neighbors realize they've been spotted.

"Is there somewhere more private we can talk?" Ef asks, reading Jovan's mind.

"Yeah, I live on the fourth floor, but..."

"But, you don't wish to invite me into your home? Understandable! We can talk in my car, no problem."

"It's not that."

"What then?"

Jovan shifts his weight from one foot to the other. "I guess I just don't understand why you want to help me. I mean, what's the catch?"

"Well, I tried explaining it to you."

"You did?"

"Yes." Ef walks to the front door leading to Jovan's apartment building. He holds the door open and leans his wide frame against it. "I want to help because that's what *Chipped for Unchipped* is all about."

The full moon lights the birch trees swaying in the gentle breeze. An owl calls out, breaking the silence of the building complex's courtyard. Jovan sits against the metal railing of his balcony. He turns to look over his shoulder, hoping to get a glimpse of the owl. Sometimes there are several of them at once, sitting in the tree that rises tall between the yellow concrete buildings.

A paper notebook lies open in front of him, a pen resting between the pages. Jovan rubs the tips of his fingers. How long has it been since he's written anything by hand? Two years? Four? Ten? For hours, he's sat on the balcony, writing these short notes, ripping off the pages, and folding them into his hardhat. These notes, spreading the message Ef had taught him earlier, could save dozens of lives.

If only his coworkers take them seriously.

He picks up the pen, shoves it between his teeth. He tears another page filled with writing, then folds it into a self-made envelope and tosses it in the hardhat. Then he starts a new note.

The chipping interviews will start tomorrow. Jovan needs to be the first one at the job site. If Dunja is the only one who listens to him—he'll take it. This sleepless night will be worth it as long as she pays heed.

The owl hoots again, startling Jovan. Cursing under

his breath, he tears a new page from the notebook. He squeezes the paper into a tight ball inside his sweaty fist.

What if Dunja won't listen either?

Jovan gets up from the balcony floor. He turns to look at the courtyard and scan the tree for owls. The hooting continues; he can't see anybody around. All the balconies are empty. All lights are off, except for the moon. The owl stays hidden, but keeps calling.

He opens his fist and straightens the paper out. The letters are now barely visible on the wrinkled paper, but they're still there. The message is too absurd to understand. To believe.

THE CHIPPED ARE NOT WHO THEY SAY THEY ARE.

PEOPLE HAVE GONE MISSING. NOT EVERYONE WILL MAKE IT.

CO-OPERATE AND DON'T ASK QUESTIONS.

The note slippery in his sweaty hand, Jovan waits for the first workers to arrive. To some, he could hand the note in person. For those he doesn't trust, he's left a note in their designated workspace. The stacks of tiles have doubled overnight. They're supposed to start installing them on the second floor today. The shipping containers that serve as offices sit quietly in the brightening morning. An owl calls out somewhere in the distance, but other than that, the only sound Jovan can hear is his own, intermittent breath.

The silhouettes of three men appear in the distance. Rumbling laughter fills the air. The man in the middle carries a black trash bag over his shoulder. He spits carelessly to his left, making the man walking with him jump aside. He doesn't tell Filip to watch where he's spitting. He continues laughing at the man's jokes as if nothing happened.

When Jovan sees Dunja arrive in the distance, he stands up and steps into the middle of the yard. In his pocket, he picks out a folded paper note, fingers its edges nervously. He won't get any papercuts; his hands are too worn and weathered for that.

"Hey," he says and nods at Filip, hoping he'll keep going and head straight for his workspace.

But Filip stops in front of him, a step too close. Jovan needs to look up to meet his gaze.

"You're in my way."

Jovan takes a deep breath. Then he steps aside and mumbles, "My bad."

"What's your problem with me anyway, man?" Filip says. "I brought your shit back. All nice and clean too, wasn't it?"

It hadn't been.

"Yeah, it's not that. It's all good."

Filip spits next to Jovan's shoe and chews on something in his mouth. "What is it, then?" More spit.

Jovan stares at Dunja, gathering her stuff from the back of her truck. The note shakes slightly in his sweaty hand.

This time Filip's spit lands on the shipping container's metal wall. "The fuck's this? A love letter? Aww, you shouldn't have."

The two men chuckle, exchanging a look with each other behind Filip's back.

"Gotta tell you, Josefina... Clean freaks are really not my thing."

He won't get it back. Filip won't believe the message in it either. But he has to try. "Read it, then burn it after. I know it's a lot to take in but the interviews—"

"Morning, fellas." The job site supervisor Luka appears from behind a shipping container. "What's this little meeting all about?"

Filip keeps his eyes on Jovan. "Nothing, sir." He turns and tosses the folded paper on the ground. "Abso-fucking-lutely nothing." The black trash bag rustling on his shoulder, Filip stomps away, whistling a tune. The two men turn to follow him.

Before his supervisor has a chance, Jovan picks the note up and shoves it back into his pocket. His hand is wet with Filip's saliva.

"What was that all about?" Luka asks, nodding at the men as they walk off into the distance.

"Nothing, sir."

"Didn't look like nothing to me."

Jovan thinks, desperate to come up with a good lie. "Fundraising," he says. "Yeah, my girlfriend's sister's dog needs surgery. I know we're not supposed to collect CC's around the site, sir, but she wouldn't leave it alone."

"A dog surgery?"

Jovan spreads his hands. "Crazy times, am I right?"

Luka shakes his head and opens the shipping container's door. "I'll say." Before he closes the door behind him, he pops his head out. "Don't forget," he says. "The ChipReps will be here in half an hour. Let the other assholes on the floor know too."

Half an hour? Jovan swallows and wipes his hand clean inside his pocket. "Sir, I thought the interviews didn't start until lunchtime."

Luka shrugs and steps into his office. The door flaps shut behind him.

"Shit, shit, shit…"

Jovan starts running toward the parking lot. He needs to catch Dunja before she gets to the site. He picks out a folded paper, one that hasn't been swimming in Filip's snot.

"Hey, egghead!" Dunja greets Jovan and leans in to grab her hardhat, toolkit, and lunchbox from the car's trunk. "Bright and early, are we?"

Jovan shoves the paper into her hands. "Dunja, you must read it. Read it twice." Jovan looks over his shoulders. Black SUVs and vans have started to appear in the parking lot. "We don't have much time."

"A note? Why didn't you just message me?"

"No, no. No digital messages. Not about this."

"Jovan, what's gotten into you?"

"Please, Dunja." He grabs her by the shoulders. "Just read it. Please."

Her eyes linger on Jovan for a while. Then she unfolds the paper and starts reading. A frown shadows her face. She looks up from the paper, shaking her head. Then she reads the note again. "This doesn't make any sense," she says. "What do you mean, 'not all will make it'?"

"It's all fucked up, Dunja. The city will pick and choose people to be part of this Happiness-Program."

She huffs. "Are you high?"

"No, Dunja, I'm not high. I'm dead serious. The people running this city are murderous fucks. Just trust me on this."

"Murderous? What has made you so paranoid all of a sudden? You sure you're right about this?"

Jovan takes the note from her and shoves it back into his pocket. "Would you rather be right," he says, "or would you rather stay alive?"

Installing one tile after another, Jovan works on the second floor. But his mind is elsewhere. He's picked the side of the building where he can see the shipping containers where the interviews are being held. Five people have been called in. None of them have exited the offices' front doors and gone back to work. In the parking lot, one black vehicle after another drives to the back side of the boxy offices, but Jovan can't see what happens there. Do the offices have backdoors? Another van turns and drives out to the parking lot and then onto the road.

Luka circles the yard, looking down at an electric pad in his hands. "Filip?" he calls out. "You're next!" The rugged man filled with spit and punches makes his way to the first office and walks in. The door flaps shut behind him.

Dunja's already in. She's been called into the third office. She hasn't come out either, but no black vehicle has driven to the third box.

Should Jovan run? Escape? Where would he go? The city is the only place with a functioning society. The countryside and suburbs have fallen quiet. Nobody seems to know where the people have gone. The only explanation given by the authorities is that most people stay inside now. Working from home, getting used to living in an alternate reality, as they should. Children and teens are encouraged to study in AR-realities, learn basic coding, software development, and AR-world building, so they'll become useful individuals and have good jobs when they grow up. Food and medicine deliveries and 3D printers have emptied the grocery stores and pharmacies of walk-in customers.

It's a ghost town. It has been for a while now. But somehow the city still builds, offering more construction jobs than there are workers available.

Is that a skill, Jovan? Being a construction worker?

Hardly.

Luka takes a few steps toward the job site, tapping on the pad. "Jovan? Come on down!" he yells. "You're next!"

Jovan puts down the hardhat and his pull bar and takes the stairs down. Then he starts toward the offices.

He *should* run. In the opposite direction.

Buy some time.

Expose the Chipped and their beyond-questionable morals.

Jovan's almost at the offices when the door flies open. Filip comes out running, screaming words Jovan can't make sense of. He runs toward Jovan, waving his hands wildly in the air. A man steps out of a black SUV and aims a gun at Filip. A dart whooshes through the air and lands in Filip's shoulder. He falls down on the ground.

The SUV glides up slowly next to him. Luka hurries to Jovan, grabs his shoulder to lead him toward the offices. "I know, I know. Looks bad, doesn't it?" Luka says. "But it's not what you think. Filip's been having these episodes for some time now. Today, we simply suggested he should see someone once a week and that he should start taking his medicine." Luka stops by the door, now off its hinges after Filip lunged through it. "I guess that was enough to push him over the edge."

"Episodes?"

"Mm." Luka nods. "Schizophrenia."

Horseshit. All of it. So Luka's in on it.

Jovan looks over his shoulder to see three men, dressed in camo coveralls, drag Filip into the back seat of a car with tinted windows. Luka clears his throat, keeping the shipping container's door open for Jovan. "Shall we?"

There's nowhere to go. He'll have to just play this right. Lie.

Just as Jovan is about to step into the windowless office, he's momentarily blinded by the sun. Early morning beams reflect off of something tossed on top of a trash barrel by the third office.

Something blue. Metal.

A lunchbox.

Minnie Mouse smiling on its side.

"Have a seat, Jovan," the woman on the screen says. Her white lab coat and friendly smile send a cold wave through Jovan's body. Her accent is barely there, but enough so for Jovan to know she's not a local. A man dressed in blue coveralls stands in the dimly lit office corner. He's fidgeting with a machine, his back turned toward Jovan.

Jovan sits on a metal stool in the middle of the room, facing the screen on its stand. Hands in his pockets, he fingers the note he showed Dunja in the parking lot.

"My name is Doctor Niinistö, and I'm here on the behalf of the Solomon Foundation" the woman on the screen says. "I will be interviewing you today. Just a basic procedure, no need to be nervous."

The man in blue coveralls walks over and motions for Jovan to take off his hardhat.

"Mikko here will be assisting me today. You don't mind wearing a wired hat and a wrist bracelet for a few minutes, do you?"

Yes. I mind. Any normal human being would.

"Of course not," Jovan says. He tries to keep his voice light. "What are they for, exactly?"

Mikko brings over a hat with small electrodes and wires attached to it. He hands it to Jovan. While Jovan puts the hat on, Mikko holds a metal bracelet out in his extended hand. He taps his feet on the floor and sighs loudly.

"They're your first chance to try out some chip technology. The hat and the bracelet measure your body temperature and other functions. Think of it as a basic health exam when entering a new job."

A lie detector. That's what this is. Shit.

"Cool."

The woman on the screen laughs. "Agreed. It is phenomenal what technology can do these days."

Once Jovan has tucked the hat on, he finally extends his hand for the bracelet. With a single movement, Mikko snaps it on, turns on his heels, and returns to the corner to stare at the flickering machine. He puts on a set of AR-glasses that blink a blue light.

"Shall we begin?"

Jovan's sweaty fingers tear into the paper note inside his pocket. "Ready when you are."

"Is your name Jovan Buha?"

"Yes."

"You live and work in the City of Serbia?"

"Or Belgrade," he says. "I mean—yes."

So far, so good. But something tells Jovan the

questions will soon become much more specific than this.

The hat doesn't make any sounds. The bracelet on his wrist reflects neon-blue light and buzzes quietly.

"Have you ever broken the law, Jovan?"

His hand stops fiddling with the hidden note. His face is hot, burning. Sweating is the last thing he should do when plugged into a lie detector. "Umm. Yes. I guess I have."

"What was your crime?"

"I sold stolen goods on the black-market, but only for a while. Until I found a job in construction."

Is that it? Will he now be labeled as a rebel? An outlaw? Will they stuff him into a barrel of trash, and leave him there to rot next to a Minnie Mouse lunchbox?

"I see. And when was this?"

"Eight... no, eleven years ago."

The woman falls silent, still staring at Jovan and smiling. He stares back, thinking that it's somehow a part of the test. If he folds and moves his gaze first, Doctor Niinistö will wave a hand, and in will come the soldiers.

After a minute, maybe two, Mikko nods from the corner. Doctor Niinistö takes a sip of water before she continues.

"Do you currently have suicidal or violent thoughts?"

She's still asking questions. The interview continues.

Jovan might not end up rotting in a dumpster after all.

"No, I don't."

"Have you ever had suicidal or violent thoughts?"

The paper tears more in his hands. A drop of sweat lands on his lap.

"I don't… I guess everyone has. Don't you think?"

Don't ask questions. Don't make comments. Just get through this alive.

The doctor's smile deepens. "I think you are absolutely right, Jovan," she says. "I know I have violent thoughts all the time."

His heart rate races. *Shit.*

"But it doesn't mean that I would act on those thoughts," Doctor Niinistö says, smiling. "Does it now?"

Jovan swallows and gives her a nod. The room is now spinning. His nerves are about to give out. He feels like screaming. He wants to rip off the wired hat, destroy the bracelet, and run out the broken door. He wants to burn the Chip-Center down—burn the whole city—and curse every single being who's involved in the Happiness-Program.

He wants to fight for his freedom. For his right to choose.

Mikko nods again from the other side of the room. Doctor Niinistö lifts her gaze and then her chin. Maybe to check the time on a clock nearby. Or maybe to send Mikko some secret command. Doesn't matter. All Jovan can do is wait.

“Well, okay then,” Doctor Niinistö says. Her eyes drill into Jovan’s, the smile that seems to be stuck on her face suddenly fades away. “One last question. Then we’ll let you get back to work.”

He’s been honest this whole time. They don’t care about his criminal record. They’re letting him go back to work. The hat’s still on, and he hasn’t burst out screaming. He still stands a chance.

“What’s your take on the Happiness-Program, Jovan?”

Shit. Shit. Shit. Shit.

He takes a deep breath and closes his eyes. He thinks of Dunja. Even Filip. He thinks of all the people who haven’t made it through this test. Would there be others? People hiding in the woods or at the abandoned harbor? People who are now hunted, for no good reason. People who would need his help.

But how can he help if he has no power? If he’s not someone important?

“I support the program,” Jovan says, the words coming out slow but steady. “I support it one hundred percent.”

“And you’ll happily be a part of it?”

“I will,” he says. “I’m going to be a soldier. Here, in the City of Serbia.”

“Really? And why is that?”

His breath eases. His heart rate stays steady. He lets go of the paper, hidden deep in his pocket, knowing his message will never again see daylight. Jovan smiles at the woman who has just stolen his freedom.

"Because it's the best thing to do. For anyone who wants to stay alive."

4

LUNA

February 2089
East-Land, City of Serbia

CHAPTER 1
4 IN THE MORNING

Drops of blood stain the trail of soggy brown leaves. In the headlamp's light, she considers each step, careful not to place her hiking boots on the slippery roots that poke out of the forest floor. She can't risk slipping and falling—not if she wants to catch this thing before sunrise.

She continues deeper into the sleepy woods. A nightjar's whistling call splits the morning air. A churring sound follows. Luna continues her trek through the waking forest, her new shoes slightly too visible and bright even in the dim morning light. Neither her luminous footwear nor the headlamp wobbling on her forehead are likely to matter. The elastic band needs adjusting again. But now is not the time; she's getting close.

The trace of blood disappears by a fallen spruce tree. Cursing under her breath, Luna drops the rucksack from her back and sets the plastic carrier on the ground.

Did she bring the right box? Or will this beast be too large to fit in the one she brought?

"Doesn't really matter if I can't find you, does it?" she mumbles into the collar of her jacket. She kneels down and opens a zipped pocket at the side of the rucksack. Her stomach won't be happy about this liquid breakfast, but she's forgotten her food pouch near the pen again. One of these days, she'll have to bother the Reverend to fix that jammed gate.

Hot coffee burns her throat, but she continues to take one gulp after another. This is all the refreshment she's brought with her from the farm. If she doesn't hydrate, she'll get a nasty cramp in one of her calves... or possibly both. Coffee isn't great for hydrating, but it's better than nothing.

The fallen tree trunk makes an uncomfortable seat, but Luna sits down anyway. Steam rises from the thermos she's holding. She would almost prefer to hear the *whoosh* of a tranquilizer dart or a neon-light grenade landing nearby with a *clink*. Sounds of the woods are nearly as disturbing as the sound of war. She's become so accustomed to the way the Chipped have altered the world, that nature's whispers now seem almost unnatural. Untrustworthy. But it's the city people who can't be trusted, hunting down all of Luna's kind.

Right now, her enemy is sound asleep. They shouldn't get the best of both worlds; their privileged new life *and* their full night of rest.

But it'd be foolish to think they'd have to choose.

The city takes what it wants, and then it takes more. The Chipped destroy those who think differently from them, collecting what they assume to be theirs—rightfully or not. Their darts strike down anyone who carries a damaged brain implant, taking them one at a time.

A faint whimper snaps Luna out of her dreary thoughts. She turns off her headlamp and sits quietly. Ears ringing in the silence, she wishes she could use a set of AR-glasses with their body heat detector app. Too bad the Reverend now locks all the Chipped technology in his garage.

The whine gets louder. Luna reaches for the sack and pulls out a blanket. She bundles the fabric under her arm and creeps toward the sound. Beyond the fallen spruce tree, the ruins of an old building sleep among the moss and weeds. The crying seems to be coming from underneath a pile of collapsed boards. Luna unfolds the blanket and gets closer. Then she kneels down and continues on all fours. Her pants are soaked from the knees down, but she barely notices. Her eyes lock on the whimpering creature, resting in a forgotten nook in the middle of a collapsed world.

"Here, buddy-buddy," she says, hoping the thing won't take off running. Considering how easy the blood trail was to follow, the animal's injury won't be just a scratch or a strain. The whining stops, but the bundle of fur stays put. Luna places the blanket over the shaking dog.

Now she waits.

In the dark, the silhouette of the injured hound looks tiny. With a soft voice, Luna continues to talk to it. It's unlikely it'll run away now, but it might still bite her if she picks it up too soon.

"Did you stumble on a trap, Buddy? Is it ok if I call you Buddy?"

The blanket shakes with the dog's rapid breathing.

"Shitty. And completely useless. They'll never catch a thing with that kind of junk."

The tip of a snout digs out of the blanket. Sniffing, shaking, the dog listens to her words. It hasn't shown its teeth. But not all of them are aggressive—until you try and carry them away.

"Good news is, there's not many of us left to build those traps. Just a handful of Unchipped suckers left, Buddy. Soon it'll just be you guys. And once that happens, you won't have to worry anymore."

A pair of ink-black eyes peeks out from under the blanket. The weary look on the dog's face makes Luna want to chuckle and cry—both at the same time.

"Well, hello there. I'd offer you some turkey jerky, but I left it by that damned gate. I guess that's the bad news this morning."

She shouldn't bring this dog home. It'd be the fifteenth "buddy" she'd dragged onto the premises. And each time she brings in a new stray, the Reverend raises the rent by 20 CC's. Money's not a problem: Two or three hours on her chip-pad will bring her more than she can spend. But she doesn't want to steal from the city's tenants forever. And to hack into the Solomon Foundation's money is a whole other cyber-game.

In the distance, a flock of drones rises with the morning's first sunbeams. The time for beauty sleep is over. The hunt is back on. And what the drones are after has nothing to do with abandoned, once-domestic animals. They *are* looking for strays, though—the ones with two feet.

"Time to go, Buddy," Luna says as she stands up. The dog's head tilts as she makes her way over. "If you bite me, I'll bite you back." Her arms wrap around the blanket and lift the dog up. Its head dives back into the sheet, but no teeth sink into Luna's flesh.

Her white boots now less white, she makes her way back to the fallen spruce tree. With the drones now scanning the area, she'll need to stay off the trail. Moving through the thick woods with a heavy rucksack and a sizable carrier is not ideal, but neither is getting a tranquilizer dart in her neck.

"Almost there, Buddy." She feels something wet on her hand and wrist. The injury is bleeding again. But this is not the time or place to tend to it.

Back on the trail, she places the dog in the carrier and closes the door. She digs for her inhaler in one coat pocket. Then the other. Then the rucksack's side pockets. But it's not there.

"Such a scatterbrain..." she mumbles, throwing the rucksack back on.

A dull pressure behind her head tells her the Reverend is awake. Most likely, he's lost one of his precious belongings; his reading glasses, the raincoat for his coveralls, the ketchup bottle. As usual, Luna refuses to open the telepathic connection between them. Why does the man keep tapping her after two years when she hardly ever answers? Maybe it's just an alarm system. Or maybe he just likes knowing she's out there. She can understand that. Just like Luna's dogs, she can't resist the human connection, no matter how many wrong buttons the Reverend tends to push. Instead of tapping, she chooses to walk from the attached guest house to the main house.

"Let's get you home, Buddy."

She swipes at a loose strand of hair, smudging something warm onto her face. Her face, coat sleeves, and hands covered in blood, Luna picks up the carry-on and steps off the trail. Breath wheezing, she hopes the drones lack microphones. They might soon spot the fresh blood on the trail, but Luna should be long gone by that point. Mostly the drones are looking for movement. Only a few of them can spot tracks or detect bodily fluids.

A movement on the trail. Luna ducks down into the Lilac and Smoke tree shrubs. The carrier lands too hard and makes the dog cry out in pain.

Crap, crap, crap.

A man. Her age, maybe a few years older. Wearing purple coveralls and thermo-boots. Luna checks his belt for a dart-gun but can't see one. Maybe he's not a soldier? The city soldiers travel in packs, not alone. And they wear camouflage coveralls, not the city's regular outfit. But if not a soldier—what is a Chipped person doing this far from the city at this hour?

The man makes his way to the fallen spruce. He kneels down and dips his fingers in the puddle of blood on the ground. Then he gets up and looks around, scanning the woods. Luna presses herself against the carrier where the dog remains buried under the bloodstained blanket. A faint whimper muffles the ringing in Luna's ears.

"Hello?" the man calls out. His voice is calm, friendly. But just like with every other human being left on the planet, his looks could be deceiving. "I'm not going to hurt you. Not that you'll believe that… Hey, is this yours?"

Ha. Nice one, Luna thinks, keeping her head low, forcing herself to stay calm.

"Still has some coffee left," he calls out. "Oh, and an inhaler." A puffing sound echoes from the trail. "With puffs left and everything."

Her wheezing suddenly seems louder. Who is this chip-skull to hold her inhaler hostage? The damn thing is nearly impossible to come by these days. The Reverend has run out of excuses for needing one so she's been trying to make this one last. He might not be appropriately Chipped, but he does have access to the city's health care.

"I can hear you gasping."

More aggravated than frightened, Luna sits up in the bushes. The man doesn't have a dart-gun with him. She knows this because if he did, the first thing he would have called out would have been a lie telling her he was unarmed.

Without a word, she makes her way back to the collapsed tree and her belongings. Heart beating against her chest, she walks straight up to the guy and snatches the inhaler from his hand. After a much-needed puff, she reaches for the thermos, but the amused man hides it behind his back.

"Whoa, hey," he says. "I can see that I've upset you. That's not my intention at all. And I'm not like the others—" Her scoff interrupts his words. "Yeah, I know. I get it. Why would you ever believe me." After a pause, he peeks at Luna from under his brows. "What's your name?"

Luna folds her arms on her chest and takes a step closer. "None of your business, asshole. That's my name." Every inch of her body wants to run away, but she forces herself to stare the man down. No trace of a gun. No AR-glasses on. But what is he doing here, if not hunting the Unchipped?

"Should I just call you Toots?"

"Do that, and you'll find that thermos so deep in your throat that a thousand inhalers won't save you."

Another pause. He investigates Luna's face, clearly unsure how to proceed. "I really didn't mean to upset you like this."

"Then give me back my coffee, and we'll go our separate ways?"

"I'm afraid your coffee's all gone," he then says, smiling carefully. "Got thirsty while waiting for you to quit your game of hide-and-go-seek." What the fuck. Jokes? Who in the world thinks they can lighten the mood right now?

"Whatever. Just give me the bottle."

"And where are you going, with that heavy-ass carrier? Covered in blood? It's not even breakfast time, and you already look like you've been dragged across a pile of corpses."

Why does he think he has the right to know this? Or is that a threat? If it is, it's an odd one. Everyone knows the Chipped never kill the outcasts. Their bodies are much more useful when they're still alive.

"What's it to you?" Luna says. When the man doesn't reply, Luna reaches out her hand. "Please?"

After hesitating for a few seconds, the man grabs Luna's extended hand, shaking it firmly. Luna's heart races against her chest, not sure if it's because of rage or fear. This fucker is *touching* her now?

She pulls her hand back. "Are you insane? What the hell?"

"Hey, whoa. Sorry! I can see that you're nervous, but I assure you I'm not going to hurt you. I'm just here surveying the land," he says, quickly placing the thermos in her hand. "I'm Jovan. City of Serbia's proud land surveyor."

Why on earth would she care what this psycho's name is? And is he expecting her to tell him what her name is? Is he completely clueless?

Luna presses her belongings against her chest, hesitant to turn her back on him. If he was planning to attack her, he probably would have done so already. Unless he's playing with his prey, luring and teasing. Maybe it's something he's learned from the AR-games they play in the city.

"I better get going," she says and takes a few steps backward, keeping her eyes on the man's hands. They hang at his sides, playing with the coverall's rain cover.

"Don't forget to pick up your friend."

Luna stops on the trail, her hands closing into fists. Is he after the dog? And here she thought the black-market's meat business was a thing of the past, with most of Serbia's Unchipped captured.

"You want it?"

"Do I want what?"

"The damn dog. Seems rabid. Foaming mouth and all."

He chuckles and rubs his chin.

"No, I don't want it. Rabid or not. You know, there's a sanctuary for animals. Just outside the city gates."

"Oh, I'm sure there is," Luna calls out and starts walking. If he's going to shoot her, now would be the time. If a drone drops a neon-bomb on her, it should land any second now. But all she hears is the steady ring of silence.

"Hey, Bloody Mary!"

She stops by the small trail of her own footsteps. Only a few feet away lies a wounded being, desperately needing medical care.

"What?"

"They're sending drones deeper inland. Not to catch your kind, but to map out the area."

"Map it out for what?"

"Expansion. The city needs more space for farming. Construction will start soon."

Of course it needs more. More space. More brainwashed people. More power.

"And you're telling me this because?"

He shrugs and pulls out a pair of AR-glasses from his coverall pockets. Will there be a dart-gun too?

But he steps over the spruce tree, tapping into the air. A smile lingering on his face, he calls out one more time.

"Because I figured you deserve to know. You're the last Unchipped to have survived the war."

CHAPTER 2
THE DOG PEN

The Reverend leans closer to the mirror, investigating the lines underneath his eyes. Crosslegged, Luna sits in the middle of the main house's kitchen table, surrounded by medicine bottles, syringes, bandaids, and gauze.

"Would it kill you to sit on a chair once in a while? Like a normal person?" her landlord asks. Luna's habit of sitting on tables and counters has always made him huff and puff.

"What's it to you, where I sit?"

He mumbles and waves her off, returning his gaze to the mirror in front of him and away from his obnoxious tenant.

"One day… I'm telling you, Lu. One day these damn things are going to mold right into my face."

A set of AR-glasses hangs from his neck, blinking and shining a purple light.

"Look at the bright side, Marić," Luna says, reading

another leaflet about expired medicine, "They cover most of your ugly mug."

"Do they now..." Reverend Marić mumbles, spreading lotion under his eyes. The pills the city gives him help with the pain. But only some. His damaged chip continues to fight against the AR-glasses. "They also make me seasick. Have I told you that?"

"Only every thirteen seconds, or so."

"Don't be a wise-ass, Lu."

"Beats whining like a bitch."

Reverend Marić sets the AR-glasses on the bureau in the front hallway. He might be used to the pain from the blinking lights, but not everyone is; Luna would rather be mauled by a wolf than put any kind of Happiness-Program technology on her face.

As Marić opens the fridge, the room is filled with the sound of claws clicking against the tile floor. A yellow mutt makes its way to the Reverend. By the open refrigerator, the dog sits and tilts its head.

Shit.

"How many fucking times do I have to tell you?"

Luna jumps off the table. "Sorry, Marić." She hurries to the dog and grabs it by the scruff of its neck. "Won't happen again."

"Mmm. Sure. And I'll stop drinking moonshine and ignoring the fact that you're three days late on rent. Again."

"Wacko, come," Luna calls for the dog as she heads to the door that leads to her side of the farmhouse.

Telling Marić she'll pay him soon would only make the moody man moodier. She closes the door to her open-space apartment and ties it shut with a length of rope.

"Seriously, Wacko," she mumbles to the yellow mutt. "Touch that rope again, and we're all homeless."

Wacko tilts his head and then bolts off and out the open screen doors. Outside in the dog pen, a dozen dogs bask in the midday sun. The yard is filled with the carcasses of broken cars, old furniture, and other debris. A junkyard. That's what it looks like, not a place where people eat, sleep, and hope to live another day. If the drones were to buzz their way over here, they would have a hard time spotting the dogs among all the junk. So far, they've left this area alone, knowing that the Reverend would report any loitering around his place of residence. Or that's what his employers in the city think, anyway.

Luna plops down on the mattress by the fireplace and looks around; towers of paperbacks and hardcover books, bundles of dirty clothes, bloody towels, half-eaten packages of vegan cookies and chocolate bars. The inside of her home looks just as cluttered as the outside.

Empty plates and travel mugs lie around the floor, licked clean and shiny. With the dogs around, Luna doesn't have to worry about rats and other scavengers. Even if the doors to this place are shut with flimsy things like pieces of rope and duct tape, at least it's dry and protected from critters.

She clicks the switch on a string of Christmas tree

lights. They surround the mattress, providing just enough light for her to read by. Fortunately there's electricity. It comes with rent, just like the water. Not that she'd ever drink out of a faucet. Not after Marić told her what had happened to the City of England.

On a good day, the Reverend brings Luna things from the city. Sometimes Luna pays for them, sometimes she doesn't. She's not sure why the man keeps her around. Why he hasn't dragged her ass to the city, planted her in a stasis capsule, and shut her off for good. For the longest time, Luna thought it was because of Marić's wife, Sloboda. Until her dying day, the woman was filled with good intentions and kind ideas. Sloboda's the one who offered Luna shelter and let her take in her first strays. It took Luna a long time to trust her. And once she did, Luna didn't know how to tell her so. She just hoped that Sloboda knew.

Sloboda's been dead for half a year now. Withered away by brain cancer and her unwillingness to try any healing options the Chipped had to offer.

She shakes her head, trying to get rid of her thoughts about the dreadful day when she dug a hole for the only person she still cared for. Luna reaches for her laptop. Neon code runs along the screen: adware she worked on last night. Though her fingers tingle and her eyes devour the numbers, Luna has no time for the Chip-Charity hack. She'll need to put in some serious work—actual work—to get Marić paid on time. Or at least Luna's "on time"—five days late.

One of these days Marić will have had enough of her. He'll abandon her, just like everyone else in Luna's life has. The least she can do is stop giving the grumpy old fart more reasons to do so.

Moonlight throws deep shadows around the dump that is Luna's backyard. The dogs are all inside, sleeping side by side on her mattress, no doubt. Luna sits on top of an old rusty Opel—what's left of it—its doors ripped off and tires flat against the muddy ground.

The laptop rests face down, propped open on its edges. She looks, searching for the stars. The clouds move fast, blocking and revealing the glimmer of the night sky. The T-shirt and pajama pants are enough to keep her warm in the mild winter night. It won't be cold until it gets late. That's the time when she usually roams in the woods, looking for creatures abandoned by their families or orphaned in The Great Affliction. Beings that will never be able to pay her back for her trouble. But it's not the dogs Luna intends to make her money from.

She will stay put tonight. Sleep in tomorrow morning. Her new buddy's wound needs tending every two hours or so. The foothold trap in the woods chopped off a piece of his hind leg. The injury is not grave, but she needs to keep it from getting infected. And Luna needs to keep the dog tucked away behind the storage boxes. She will get rent on time, but only if

Marić doesn't spot the newcomer and raise the amount by another twenty CC's.

The adware runs a new code, the laptop's fans whirring wildly. Hacking into the Chip-Charity was never supposed to be easy, but Luna's frustrated by how well the Chipped have built their firewalls. And it's not surprising; they've recruited the best of the best. And not just programmers, but farmers, biologists, doctors, scientists, and mechanics. Anyone with a true talent is welcome to join them in the purple city. Or maybe Luna was never welcome, because of her parents' activity against the program. Either way, these people had put her through something she never volunteered for.

Footsteps by the barbed wire fencing. The sound snaps Luna out of the horror that is her past. Marić tries to open the jammed gate. Luna's food pouch lies next to the entrance, still full and forgotten. Her modest stash of imported root beer and ginger ale, along with the cookies and chocolate, has been enough to keep her satisfied. And it should; one can of soda on the black-market—if such a thing still exists, Luna's not sure—would cost her a month's rent.

"I thought I fixed this piece of crap?" Marić lifts the metal latch, but it stays stuck on the fence's wooden frame.

Luna reaches for her laptop, flips it around, and shuts the lid. "You did. Six months ago."

"And you broke it again?"

"The wood swells in the rain. It needs a new latch."

"Why didn't you tell me?" The latch finally gives in, sending Marić stumbling backward. He trips on a partly rotten chicken cage and lands on his ass. "Stupid piece of shit."

Luna hides the laptop under her T-shirt. "You okay there, old fart?"

Marić makes his way into the pen and digs out a vape. "Mind your business, whippersnapper," he mumbles. "You'll be lucky if you look half as good when you are my age."

"You call that mug of yours good-looking? Please."

"Half good-looking. Your generation truly is terrible at listening. Shiny, blinking, glimmering things are all you think of. Your own voice the only thing you hear."

Luna swallows her words, biting her thumbnail. It's not uncommon for the Reverend to get sidetracked like this, forgetting Luna's state in life. Nothing in this junkyard blinks or shines. Her voice hasn't been heard by anyone but him for over two years. Not really. She barely talks to anyone but the dogs.

The Reverend circles the Opel carcass, kicking its flat tires. "I remember when you found this piece of junk."

Luna smiles and hugs her legs against her chest. She gazes up at the racing clouds. "I do too. You had three mufflers waiting for me on the kitchen table the very next morning."

Marić's low laugh is stifled by his vape. "Did you

ever pay for that thing, anyway?"

"Oh, I paid for it, you cheap fuck. Cleaned every damn chicken coop Sloboda had. More than twenty if I remember right."

He turns away to hide his face. *Luna, you moron*, she thinks to herself. She should know better than to bring up her name.

The Reverend climbs into the Opel's passenger seat. Vaping quietly, he stares into space while Luna—still sitting on top of the rusty roof—counts the distant stars. On nights like these, her landlord used to bring out the moonshine and two crystal glasses. Sloboda's finest. They'd sit in silence and fill their empty stomachs with too much booze. Then Marić stopped bringing out the glasses. Maybe they reminded him of Sloboda too much. Or maybe he was afraid he'd run out of moonshine. Luna never asked.

"How's the Chip-Charity doing this month anyway?" Luna asks, partly to break the ringing in her ears, partly because she's dying to know.

"Oh, it's all gone to shit. Ever since Kinship Care went under. Some days I wonder why they still keep me around. Why not just shove me in a capsule and call it a day."

"They could fix you."

"Like one of your Dobermans?"

"Like one of the former Unchipped, living in the city."

Marić sucks on his vape pen, blowing out a thick

cloud of smoke. Luna watches it rise on both sides of the car's roof. It makes her feel like dancing.

"That's an urban legend, I'm afraid. They've made some progress on it, but so far the Unchipped they've *fixed*," Marić pauses and makes quotation marks, "haven't made it through the operation. No, I'm better off like this. At least if you ask them. Someone needs to contact the Unchipped and keep the charity going."

The Reverend works for the Chipped, but ever since he learned the methods behind the CC's collected by the Chip-Charity he's in charge of, his heart hasn't been in it. Luna can tell. Because ever since the Kinship incident, the man's been drinking like a sponge. After the videos of plague victims turned out to be as fake as the pets and neon-colored plants, a new wave of Chipped had left City of Serbia and other AR-cities. The rebel gangs were growing all over, as was Marić's self-loathing and regret. Now, it's like he's sabotaging his own work and his status in the city.

Either the Unchipped around the City of Serbia all fled inland, or they were captured. Luna hopes it's the first option. Maybe they now live somewhere around the abandoned suburbs of the City of Germany or Belarus. Luna doesn't know. She never worries about the rebels or their plans. Why would she? Instead, she focuses on those whose fault it is they had to abandon their homes and lives here: the head of the Happiness Program, for example.

Stealing from the Chipped is too easy. Ordinary

citizens hardly keep up with their firewalls and virus protection. Hacking into a regular CC account doesn't take Luna many hours. And the harm she does is next to nothing; the people in the city barely need the money they make at the Server-Center. Plugging in for eight hours a day gets them twenty CC's, but all their necessities are covered by the government, also known as the Happiness-Program. Every now and then, they may buy a new outfit or a set of hairstyles from the AR-store, but other than that, the Chipped's bank accounts are hardly ever used.

Still, Luna feels a sting in her chest whenever she successfully draws funds from these accounts. She never empties them, not entirely. Just takes a few CC's from each account, leaving the city tenants unaware of the theft that has happened right under their AR-glasses. But the more accounts Luna needs to hack, the more manual labor it takes. She's still forty CC's short on this month's rent.

The ruined Opel shakes under Luna. The Reverend has put away his vape and is about to hit the sack. "I'm off to get some z's, kiddo," he says. "Keep those hounds out of my kitchen."

"Will do." Luna presses the warm laptop against her stomach. It's getting chilly outside. Closer to midnight. "Marić?"

"No, you can't have more time. It's not like a lightning strike, Lu. Rent is rent. It happens every month."

"It's not that. And you'll get your money. First thing tomorrow morning."

They both know that means two more days.

Marić stops by the broken gate. "What is it then?"

"Have you ever thought of changing teams?"

"Like becoming a homosexual?"

Luna rolls her eyes at him. "No, you blockhead."

"What then? Becoming an atheist? You know this reverend business is bull crap, Lu. But England wasn't the last place with religious people. Someone has to run the show."

She shouldn't approach this subject. If the Reverend ever found out about her trying to hack into his work—trying to rob his employer—he wouldn't just kick her out. He'd personally shove her ass into that stasis capsule.

"How much time do we have?"

Marić stops playing with the latch. With his back turned to her, he ponders her words for a good while before he steps out of the gate and jams the latch into the wooden frame with force.

"Who knows," he says. "You finally becoming a rebel, Lu? You leaving?"

Would it make you happy or sad if I did? Luna thinks, unsure what to say next. She fingers the laptop's edge. "I don't want to be labeled like that. I'm just me. Doing my thing."

"Catching stray dogs and installing adware for some shady overseas company?" Marić says. "I don't know, Lu. Maybe you *should* become a rebel. Give your life some meaning."

"My life has plenty of meaning," she says. "Just forget I asked."

She shouldn't have poked the beast. After all, she doesn't even want to know.

He starts toward the main house but then stops in the middle of the driveway. He turns back, only to change his mind and continue toward the main entrance. At the door, Marić stops with his hand on the handle. Then he turns around, mumbling and rubbing his chin. He's back at the gate before Luna has had time to get down from the car roof.

"You planning to attack the city or something? Kiddo, you know I got your back, but you and violence don't really go well—"

"Are you shitting me? Attack the city? Me and what army?"

Marić's eyes flicker around the yard, dodging her gaze. He spreads his arms in defeat. "You're an odd one, Lu. Slo..." he stops to clear his throat. "Sloboda always got you. Cared for you. She made me promise I wouldn't leave you. Said that you'd never join the city, nor would you trust another Unchipped to join you."

So that's why Luna's still here; it had been Sloboda's last wish. Her last wish to Luna was for her to take care of the grumpy Reverend. And now they're both stuck taking care of an underdog, lost in life.

"But to answer your question, Lu. Things are changing. The city is growing. The Happiness-Program is becoming more and more powerful. More often than not, people who flee end up in capsules as traitors. Or worse, they end up dead. Gunned down by a rebel or their own hand. Some starve to death. There are diseases out there. Collapsing buildings. Wildlife."

"I know all this, Marić. Just forget I asked," Luna says, waving him off. "I'm not going anywhere. I'm staying right here, hiding and surviving for however many days I've got."

Just like he does when the AR-glasses give him a raging headache, Marić holds his head between his hands, rubbing his temples with the tips of his fingers. Shaking his head from side to side, he curses in their native Serbian. Luna can't make out the words. She waits for the man to gather himself.

"You stupid, foolish little numb-wit. That's exactly what I worry about. You. Here. Rotting away like a worthless vehicle. Wake up, Lu. Look around, Kiddo."

Eyes watery, Luna looks around the dog pen but doesn't know what she's supposed to see.

"When are you going to wake up and understand that people need *people*? That you'll slowly go insane if you stay tucked away in this decomposing junkyard?"

Clearing her throat, she hopes her voice won't come out too weak. "I don't see you going anywhere either, Marić. What makes you any different?"

He lets go of his head and lowers his chin. "But I am going, Lu. Sooner than later, we both must choose."

She wakes up to a wet tongue licking the side of her face. Just like every other morning, Luna checks the time on her alarm clock, only to remember that it needs new batteries. It has needed new batteries for a while now. A week? A month? Time changes its meaning when you work, sleep, and roam the woods, always avoiding daylight.

The dogs are already outside. She can see them through the always-open sliding doors. Only Buddy has stayed in, waiting for his master to wake up.

"You need to pee, Buddy?"

Luna gets up and walks to the doorway. Five dogs run inside to greet her. Then they run over to sniff for fresh feed bowls. Just like the enormous sacks of dry food, their dishes are hidden in the pantry.

"Go pee, Buddy. And don't let them bully you, okay?"

The dog limps outside, but he favors his good leg a bit less than the day before. The antibiotics and wrapping must be doing something.

Luna opens the pantry door and takes out fifteen plastic feeding bowls. It was fool's luck the pet shop by the harbor wasn't completely emptied by the time she discovered it and broke in. Or is it breaking in if the door was already knocked off its hinges?

The dogs run in all at once. Luna spreads the bowls around the room and goes to find the limping dog outside. She checks the sky for drones before she walks out and scoops Buddy into her arms.

"All set, Buddy? Let's get you some chow."

Once the new dog is eating, Luna rummages through the kitchen sink and the counter. Dirty dishes, cereal, and cookie boxes fall over as she looks for the can of coffee.

"Come on, come on," she murmurs, desperate to get some caffeine moving through her veins. The sun is too high in the sky for it to be early morning. It must be closer to midday. When's the last time she slept for a full eight hours?

The tin can has fallen between the fridge and the broken dishwasher. Luna picks it up, opens the lid, and pulls out an empty coffee bag.

"Shocking," she says. Gazing at the door that leads to the Reverend's side of the house, she wonders if Marić will be gone for the whole day or only half of it. Most days, he leaves the city early. He can do his job from anywhere, but the Chipped prefer to see him at the office every day. "You work your ass off for these people," Marić has said time and time again, "and they still don't trust you."

Some things will never change. Not between the Chipped and Unchipped.

The rope hangs loose on the door. Wacko has been playing with it again, but only halfheartedly. If the mutt wanted the door open, it'd be open. Luna walks into the Reverend's home and closes the door behind her. If Sloboda was still here, there'd be no such thing as closed doors. Without fail, she had pushed for them all to be one happy family, no matter how many scoffs and eye-rolls she got in exchange. "When everything else in this world falls down, that's all we can do; stick together." That's what she had told Luna and Marić each night as they sat down to enjoy a meal together. How she wishes she had just nodded and smiled. Just once, she could have repaid the positivity and love Sloboda had for everyone around her.

Luna avoids looking at the chair at the end of the kitchen table, Sloboda's seat. Empty. No one dares to sit on it or move it. Just looking at it sends pain and regret through Luna's chest. Would things be different if she were still around? Would Marić finally stop working for the city? Would he continue fixing stuff around the house, prevent it from falling apart?

Luna takes a chair—not Sloboda's but another one—and steps on it to reach the higher cupboards. "Sneaky, sneaky," she whispers, rummaging through the Reverend's hidden stash of chocolate bars, cashews, and mini-bottles of booze. Sloboda had worked for the airline, the one that is now operated by the black-market. She wasn't one to steal, but when she got sent home jobless and hopeless, Sloboda had filled her pockets with anything and everything she could find on her last flight. Had they fired her because of the tumor? Or was it because she refused to get chipped and find work in the city?

Behind the tower of nut bags, Luna finally finds what she's looking for; a pack of dark roast coffee. She reaches for a bag of cashews, opens it, and pours the nuts into her mouth. Cheeks full, she chews and pours a fourth of the coffee into the empty nut bag. Marić will notice, but it should take him a while; he's is too lazy to prepare coffee properly on a stovetop. He prefers the Grab-a-Cup pouches that the city imports from West-Land, along with root beer and ginger ale.

After shoving one of the chocolate bars into the waistband of her pajama pants, Luna closes the cupboard, climbs down, puts the chair back in its place, and sneaks back to her side of the house.

She ties the rope around the door handle, then places the pot by the stove and lights the burner. There's still gas in there, but not for long. The small shed by the main house is running low on the refillable bottles. Just like most things, she hasn't asked Marić about it. His mood swings are bad enough as they are. Any little setback can send him to the moonshine bottle. And Luna's tired of dragging his passed-out ass to the couch whenever he decides to drown himself in moonshine and self-pity.

Back at the stove, she fishes a Turkish coffee pot from the mountain of cups, bowls, candy wrappers, and empty cookie packages. She pours half a bottle of water into the pot and waits.

"This is how it's done, you old fool," she murmurs to herself. "You don't deserve this coffee anyway."

She takes the pot off the stove right before the water boils. After adding two heaping scoops of coffee, she mixes it, and puts the pot back on the stove. When the coffee simmers, she removes the pot, stirs it, then puts it back on again. After rinsing out a coffee mug, she pours in the coffee and lets it sit.

Would it be safe to drink it outside? Even though it's a clear day?

She's tired of hiding. Tired of watching her every step, listening for spying drones, terrified of the sound of a vehicle nearby. Marić bikes to the city and back every day. Luna's not sure if the city doesn't trust him with a car or if it's because he'd be too drunk or hungover to drive one anyway.

She hears a beeping sound and turns back inside. The laptop by the mattress. It's either the Chip-Charity spyware, telling her it's found something, or the security camera showing her Marić returning home. The security system is terribly buggy, but it provides them with a false sense of safety. Better to spot suspicious squirrels and skylarks than to live completely oblivious to the farmhouse's surroundings.

Luna sets the coffee mug on the floor by the mattress and flips the laptop open.

"Huh…" she says, double-checking the premises. The system alerts her to movement in the main yard, but there are no birds or critters anywhere to be seen.

"Damn crows, playing with my mind," Luna says and places the laptop back on the floor. A bark from outside sends her up from the mattress in a split second.

She walks to the sliding doors and peeks outside. "Is

that you barking, Buddy?" she whispers, scanning the yard as well as she can without stepping outside. The computer beeps again. Luna walks outside, presses her back against the brick wall. She makes her way to the corner and leans down by a dwarf tree. Nobody in the front yard. Not one crow. No badgers or rats.

The dogs have gone inside. Only one set of paw-steps rustles through the weed-covered yard. The new dog limps over and presses itself against Luna's thigh. She lifts the dog up and hugs it against her chest.

It's just Marić. Good ol' Marić. He'll call out for me any second now.

Luna closes her eyes. This is ridiculous. Hiding in her own home, kneeling in the bushes. The security system is buggy as can be. A whiff of air can set it off. A butterfly landing too close to its sensors. But something feels off. And her gut is rarely wrong.

A low growl. From inside, by the sliding doors. It's Wacko. He's the only one constantly breaking the rules. The dogs are not trained to guard the house but to be quiet. To be as invisible as possible. Another growl. Wacko paws at the spot by the door where he stands, his claws clicking against the floor. Luna sneaks closer and sees the other dogs—all fourteen—gathered on her mattress. They all stare at the door that leads to the main house.

Another beep from the laptop. Luna ducks down and presses herself flat against the wall. The gravel in the driveway crunches the way it does when Marić is biking up to the farmhouse.

Marić.

Wacko barks once. Luna curses his free spirit, scolds herself for finding such a soft spot in her heart for the yellow mutt. His rebel ways will get them all killed one day.

Beep. Beep. Beep.

She closes her eyes, pretends to be invisible—a dog in hiding.

"Lu? You home?" Marić hollers from the front yard. "You better not have gone through my stash again."

But he already knows she has. She does it every single day.

The dog jumps down from her lap. Wacko leaps through the sliding door, followed by the rest of the pack. Though the Reverend couldn't care less for the hounds, they seem to adore the man. More than they adore Luna or their daily kibble. They rush to the gate, wagging their tails.

Luna gets up and waves at her landlord. "What stash?" she calls out to him, trying to hide her shaken state of mind. "We have the rats to worry about! And would it kill you to pick up a hammer and some nails? This place is rotting as fast as your face."

"We used to have a rat problem. But then you brought in your beasts."

"See? It's good to have them around. You should be thankful!"

Marić mumbles something and makes his way inside. Luna shakes her head and heads back in too. The coffee should be the right temperature for drinking now. Her paranoia is not entirely useless, after all.

She picks up the coffee mug from the floor and brings it to her lips. Perfect taste. Perfect temperature. She'd better make some more before Marić comes in to seize her ill-gotten grounds.

Luna turns around to walk back to the stovetop. Then she freezes in place, the coffee mug hovering in midair.

The rope that keeps the door shut is gone.

"And this guy… Jovan? He does what for a living?"

Marić walks in circles around the kitchen table. Around two times. Change of direction. Another two times. Back to the right again. Crosslegged, Luna sits in the middle of the table, waving her hands in the air, she tries to find the right words.

"He said he was a land marker or something," Luna says. "Or construction? I don't know. Something to do with measuring."

"You've got to do better than that, kiddo."

Luna holds her head, rubbing her temples, trying to remember. "He said the city is expanding. And that I'm the only Unchipped who survived the war."

Marić stops and stares at her, his mouth partly open. "The only one? Surely there are some in the harbor. I mean, surely; I am still here."

"They don't count you as Unchipped, Marić. You

work for them. If they didn't need you to spy on the religious Unchipped, you'd be half-robot by now."

"But he didn't try to detain you? Didn't have a gun?"

"I'm telling you, it was like the dude was having a Sunday walk in the woods."

"AR-glasses?"

"Yes."

"Soldier coveralls?"

"Just the plain purple ones."

"What the actual fuck?"

Luna hugs her legs against her chest. She reaches for her inhaler on the table and takes a puff. "Beats me. Do you think he was at the house today?"

"That system of yours is as useless as a hundred-Euro bill. It beeps day in and out. An ant would make it go off."

"It's definitely worth a hundred Euros. Maybe more."

"According to… what? The history books? No, that piece of junk is worthless."

"It'll come handy one day."

"Nonsense."

"Want to bet on it?"

"Sure, I'll bet on it. Whatever, kiddo. Can we just focus here?"

"Right. What about the missing rope? Where the hell did that thing go?"

"Be prepared to pull it out of that mutt's ass later today."

"He doesn't eat ropes, Marić. That's not how dogs work."

He waves her off, heading to the fridge. He takes out a bottle of moonshine, opens it up, and takes a sip, not bothering with a glass. "Did you check for footprints by the camera?"

Footprints. Of course. Why didn't I think of that?

"Of course I did." She clears her throat. "But it wouldn't hurt to have a set of fresh eyes."

Marić sets the bottle on the table, coughing. Then he grabs his vape and heads out the main entrance. It takes a while for Luna to get off the table and follow his tracks.

By the time Luna gets outside, Marić's already examining the camera. He investigates the wet soil. Out of breath, Luna rushes over. How the old man is in so much better shape than she continues to amaze her. It must be all the biking.

"Found anything?"

Marić gets up and steps aside. "I guess I owe you a hundred Euros," he says. "Because those are definitely not my footprints."

They sit in the rotting Opel, staring in opposite directions from one another. The argument started hours ago, by the security camera out front, and it has lasted ever since. As if by silent agreement, they've taken a break from hissing at each other. Arms folded on their chests, they stare at the sun as it's about to set.

The Reverend makes small hand gestures. He speaks with his hands, always has. It used to drive Sloboda bonkers, but he couldn't help it. "You look like the town-crazy, waving and slashing the air like that," she'd say, making Luna smile and Marić give them both a dirty look.

"Are you working right now?" Luna says, her voice sharp.

His hands stop flailing. "What?"

"I know you're not having one of your telepathic conversations. Not when we're about to be drugged and dragged into a glass-wall forever-home in a moldy basement."

"You'd be hard-pressed to find any mold in the Chip-Center."

Luna can't help it. She throws her inhaler against the windshield. It bounces back and hits Marić's cheek, then bounces off, landing somewhere in the cluttered back seat.

"Ow! You little turd!"

"Focus, would you? What the hell are we going to do?"

"I say we AR-call them. They're not monsters, Lu. Let's deal with this like adults. You said it yourself; this place is falling apart. We have to make a decision someday. Might as well be today."

"Sounds like you've already made that decision. What if I haven't? I don't want to live in the city. The

AR-reality and the pill-popping will only rot my brain."

"You'd rather stay here and become dog food?"

"I'm not staying because of the dogs."

"Ha."

"I am not. I don't trust the Chipped. Why did they have to attack us? This war is completely out of proportion. They could have let the Unchipped and the Chipless be. Live in the suburbs in peace. They weren't hurting anybody."

Marić shakes his head, brings his vape to his lips. Luna leans over, tempted to grab the vape pen and throw it at the back seat. But at the last moment she wimps out and just gives him a dirty look.

"Tell me you don't agree with their agenda. Tell me you don't think it's okay to stash people inside glass tubes like drained blood. Tell me you haven't given up."

Marić lowers his chin and closes his eyes. The AR-glasses blink in his lap, but the throbbing pain in Luna's temples might as well be because of her stubborn landlord.

"Marić. Tell me."

He spreads his arms. "Alright, alright. No, I don't agree with them. But desperate times call for desperate measures. People were killing each other, Lu. Killing themselves. They turned into smartphone-driven hermits, completely braindead and useless to society. You tell me—how is that any better?"

It's Luna's turn to look away, tongue-tied and flustered. It's true. The Great Affliction would have been the end of homo sapiens if it wasn't for the Happiness Program and the AR-cities taking people in. Controlling them, yes. But also saving them from themselves.

"Well, I'm not going into one of those hell-tubes. Not without a fight."

Marić sighs. He turns to Luna, reaches for her hand, but doesn't grab it. Touching had been Sloboda's thing. *Love* had been Sloboda's thing—not Marić's.

"Just let me take you in. Let me talk to the city leaders. You don't know what kind of a deal you can get. There's this younger girl in charge of the programming. Iris something. She always says that she needs to find another worker like her. A brain that knows numbers."

"So I should just bend over? Give in and crawl into the city with a sign that says 'Will work for food?'"

"Lu. If this guy you bumped into—"

"Fucking Jovan."

"If this fucking Jovan has reported someone living with me in the farmhouse, someone other than Sloboda, that's the end of this. You can go and squat in random houses in the harbor, but you'll always be running."

Luna bites her thumbnail, avoiding Marić's gaze. She looks at the new dog, still limping but less so, the green vet wrap waving like a little flag. Wacko stretches down, his butt in the air; a sign of playtime. They wrestle around in the debris, jumping over broken buckets and chicken coops. Two more dogs join in, the rest of them cheering on the endless game of tag.

Sloboda had loved the dogs, just as Luna does. Sloboda had loved the farmhouse. Loved Luna. Loved the Reverend. Even when they couldn't love her back the same. Everything around her had bloomed, shone, and flourished. Now, her absence feels like it's wearing down the house, the dog pen, the Reverend's willingness to fight for freedom. It destroys Luna's understanding of right and wrong.

If she wasn't able to trust someone like Sloboda, how could she trust Marić now? Trust *the Chipped*? After all the city has done?

A Doberman bitch runs to the Opel. She hops against the passenger door, poking Luna, inviting her to play. She's one of them. A pack of fourteen. No—fifteen. Buddy will pull through, just like every single dog Luna's ever rescued.

Shaking her head, she rolls her eyes at the Reverend and says, "I get it. And I get you, I do. I'm not going to judge you for wanting a better life. How could I? This place, the memories... I know it's all eating you up inside. This place is not the same now. Not without her."

Hands shaking slightly, Marić takes a puff of his vape. He nods approvingly. "Okay, good. Good, good, good."

"But no good," Luna says. "I'm not coming with you. If I need to move to the harbor, so be it. I'll leave the farm. Let the dogs go. But I'm not going to become one of them."

She pulls herself out of the car, heads back inside. Marić sits in the car, vaping and staring into space. Luna turns around at the sliding doors, wanting to say something witty. To make him smile, even if it's just a fake grin. Marić's smile rarely reaches his eyes anymore. Not after they set the gravestone up behind the house and filled in the hole.

One of the dogs—Tiny—jumps into the Opel. She sits on the passenger seat, staring at the grumpy, vaping man. Surprised, Luna watches Marić reach his hand over and pet the dog's heart-shaped head. A happy grin spreads across her face.

"Don't you have anything else to do? You going to stand there all day staring at an old fart smoking?"

"I guess I should get some work done. Though my landlord's pretty used to me being five days late on rent."

A lopsided smile visits his face. Just for a few seconds, but Luna catches it anyway.

"Quit being a wise-ass and go make me some of that stolen coffee of yours."

Smiling, Luna makes her way to the kitchen corner. But when she peeks out of the small window by the dishwasher, her smile turns into a worried frown. This is not like him. So many things aren't; the things he says, the weight of his voice. It's all crooked, just like Sloboda's paintings in the hallway. But unlike mediocre art in tilted photo frames, Luna can't nudge Marić's mind straight.

The man is losing his will to fight. And he's one of the strongest people Luna's met in her lifetime. Maybe it's a phase? A glitch in the system? A freak anomaly, about to vanish as soon as it appears?

Marić's going to pull through. He'll rise again, sturdier, wiser.

Right?

Luna looks through the window again.

As a crying man in a corpse of a car buries his tear-smudged face into a brown dog's short coat, she forces her mind to focus: time to prepare two cups of impeccable coffee.

It's the sound of tires that wakes her up, not the rapidly beeping laptop. The dogs gather around the mattress, Wacko's low growl sending chills through Luna's pajama-covered body.

She sits up in the bed, listens to the yard. Marić's voice. Talking to someone he knows. His voice not panicked, but not pleased either.

"Here, boy. It's okay. It's okay," she whispers. Whatever is going on outside, they need to be quiet. Remain unseen. What time is it? It must be in the middle of the night. Three in the morning? Four?

The yellow mutt jumps onto the mattress and places himself between Luna and the ropeless door. There's a red brick there now to keep the door from swinging open. So far, the dogs have left it alone.

The voices move closer. Car doors thump shut. Footsteps on the gravel. *Beep, beep, beep.* Luna reaches for the laptop and closes it. Patting Wacko's head, she reaches for the hoodie she's left by the bed and pulls it on. Then a pair of hiking pants. Then her sneakers.

Footsteps echo from the Reverend's kitchen. The steps don't belong to Marić; they're too light, too catlike. The old wooden floor barely creaks under the intruder's weight. That's when Luna knows that the steps belong to whoever left their footprints by the security camera outside. It must be fucking Jovan.

Wacko lets out another low growl.

"Shh, shh."

The footsteps continue to the hallway that separates Luna's apartment from the main house. The dogs sit quietly, staring at the door. The new, injured dog climbs onto the mattress and under Luna's arm.

She watches the doorknob turn. Wacko presses his body against Luna, protecting her from the stranger that enters the room. It's a girl—a woman—younger than Luna. Hardly twenty, she estimates. Blue and white hair floats around her head like something magical, landing softly on her shoulders. Her button nose, pale skin, silvery eyebrows and eyelashes make her look like a creature from a fairytale. She's dressed in purple and green coveralls with matching, heavy-duty boots; a soldier's attire. Luna tilts her head, investigating the intruder's belt.

"Looking for this?" the girl says and pulls out a dart-gun. It was stuffed in her leather belt. "Don't worry. I'm not here to shoot you."

To get off the mattress, Luna tries to move Wacko aside. But the dog won't budge. Stuck and cornered, Luna sits and waits for the fairy-creature to make her move. When she takes a step closer to Luna and the dogs, Wacko snarls, showing his teeth.

"Nice guard dogs you got there. I've always said we needed animals in the city."

"I don't know if they'd fit in, to be honest," Luna says. "They're the most genuine, kind, decent creatures on this planet."

The fairy grins. A buzzing sound fills the room. Something blinks inside her purple and green breast pocket. When the girl pulls out the AR-glasses, Luna looks away. Her head's already dizzy with adrenaline; the blinking lights only add to her confusion.

The girl brings the glasses up to eye-level but doesn't put them on. "Yeah, this is Iris." She talks into the glasses as if they're a walkie-talkie. "Mmm. I'm at the Chip-Charity headquarters. Yup. He's in the car. Mmm. Yeah, looks like he wasn't living alone after all."

Would Luna have time to run for a knife? From the corner of her eye, she scans the clutter on the floor, wishing she'd bothered with cutlery more often. But she has always preferred eating with her hands. Fewer dirty dishes that way.

"Mmm. Yes. Mm."

Do something, she thinks. *Say something. Scream.* But

she just sits and stares. Politely waiting for the creature to finish her phone call, Luna wonders if she's here to end Luna's short but fulfilling life. What will happen to the dogs? Will Marić take care of them? Or is he in trouble as well? He must be; he's been hiding a fugitive for years.

She should tell Wacko to attack this Iris. Let him rip apart the AR-glasses and the gun. Maybe take a chunk out of Iris's leg, giving them a head start so they can run away from the farmhouse for good. But when the yellow mutt stands up on the bed, eyes locked on the invader and teeth showing, Luna wraps her arm around him and pulls him back.

"Easy, boy."

"Doctor Solomon? I better get going. Yeah. The Unchipped is not alone, either. Mmm. Dogs. Like, a bunch of them."

Could she use her laptop as a weapon? Get close enough, pretend she'll let Iris take her into the city. Then *wham*! The girl would fall to the floor, unconscious. They'd run off. Where to? That would be a new problem, for a later time.

But Luna sits. Patiently. Her body, shaken by adrenaline and fear, is smushed between two alert dogs. She watches Iris put the AR-glasses back into her pocket.

"My employer tells me you're quite the programmer, Luna." Iris takes a step closer, holding onto her dart-gun.

Luna's eyes flicker to the laptop. "Yeah? What else does she know about me? The size of my hiking boots? Food allergies?"

Iris laughs briefly. Her blue-white hair floats around her delicate face, making her look even more magical. "She knows that you'd be a great fit for the Happiness-Program. We're looking for a new programmer to help us track a missing person. More than one. Several missing persons."

The rebels. Why do they care about the Unchipped so badly? Bunch of underdogs. A crowd of nobodies.

"I'm not sure I follow. Who's missing? Where's Marić?"

"Your friend is fine," Iris says. "For now. The rest is totally up to you."

Is he my friend? Luna thinks. Marić has always been the necessary evil. Sloboda was her friend, even if she never knew. Or more like a mother. Marić's just a grumpy old man, bitter and hateful. Right? But the thought of the Chipped hurting him makes Luna's heart race. *I guess he is my friend. And not just that... He's my only friend.*

"So you're blackmailing me? Is that it? I work for you, and no one gets hurt?"

"No need to use such harsh words. It's not blackmail if you get paid. If you get an office. We'll even let you come here and feed the dogs. Not much needs to change."

A scam. It must be.

"And if I say no?"

"You won't."

"Why wouldn't I? What do I have to lose? And what makes you think I can find these missing people for you? I'm not that great of a hacker, you know."

"No? That's not what the Finance Director tells me. They've been quite impressed by your late-hour work in the City of England. Thanks to you, they realized we need more people to work on the CC accounts and cybersecurity. I'd say if anybody can find Kaarina and the rest of the rebels, it's you."

Kaarina. Marić's told Luna about the Finnish Unchipped chick who escaped the Chip-Center—not once but twice. How have they not found her yet? An organization as big as the AR-cities against a girl with a damaged brain implant? Shouldn't make for much of a challenge.

"Who's Kaarina?" Luna says, keeping her eyes on Iris's dart-gun.

A sigh. Another step closer. Iris kneels and extends her free hand, gesturing for Tiny to come over. "Here, puppy, puppy." The dog stretches its neck but doesn't move closer to sniff the stranger's hand. When Wacko barks once, Tiny backs off and joins the rest of the pack—sitting silently by the mattress.

Iris stands up and wipes her hands on the back of her coveralls. "Are you done playing stupid? Can we get going, please? It's almost five o'clock, and I have a staff meeting first thing when my actual shift begins at eight.

Just come with me now. No need to change out of your pajamas, you'll stand out no matter what. We can chit-chat more in the car."

She shoves the gun back into her belt and turns around. Luna reaches for her laptop—her only weapon—and gets up from the mattress.

"Oh," Iris says, her back still turned to Luna, "Any funny business, any attempts to hurt me or anyone else... Let's just say that Marić's work with the charity program hasn't been what we'd call *great* for a long time. Not that everyone isn't replaceable, but he's made it to the top of the list. The Reverend used to be the best of the best. And then, one day, he got sloppy."

Since Sloboda died. Since he found a new love; moonshine. Since he gave up on shaving. Showering. Eating solids. Living.

"And if I refuse to go with you?"

Another sigh. Iris kicks the wall by the door. Plaster crumbles down, leaving a new crack to match the old. Palms resting against the doorframe, she's facing away, ready to leave the dump that is Luna's home behind.

"This farmhouse. Man, must be centuries old. Ancient foundation. Ancient framing..." Iris kicks the door frame, and a large splinter of wood breaks off. "Highly flammable, I'm sure."

This fuck-face. If this isn't blackmail, Luna doesn't know what is. She takes a few steps back and shoves the laptop into the mattress. The Christmas tree lights cast shadows around the room, making the walls vibrate in an unreal way. If Iris sees Luna hiding her computer, she doesn't let on.

Luna grabs her inhaler from the floor and gets up. "Just this one job? Find the rebels, then I'm free?"

Like the soldier's word would mean anything. Chipped scum.

"That's it. Eight 'til four, until you find them. You can spend your nights here if you so desire."

"And nothing happens to Marić?"

"Nothing that isn't already happening. No."

Luna looks around the room. The dogs tilt their heads, staring at her intensely. A high-pitched whine reaches her ears, so faint that Luna doubts Iris can hear it. Iris waits by the doorway, palms pressed against the doorframe. Her body sways in a relaxed manner, back and forth, humming a tune Luna can't recognize.

Maybe going with her isn't the end of the world. Maybe she'll be able to dig deeper into the Chip-Charity software, see the firewalls and security settings from within. No more stealing money from the city tenants. Once she gets in, she can tap into the Happiness Program accounts. Millions of CC's lie there, unused, waiting. She could pay back the people she's stolen from.

"Fuck it," Luna says, out of breath. Has she just made the biggest mistake of her life?"I just need to feed the dogs before we go."

CHAPTER 3
2 YEARS EARLIER

The phone couldn't ring at a worse time. Luna's spread her lunch on the teacher's table; last night's dinner of cabbage rolls and soy steaks, iced-tea for a drink. If she answers now and it's one of the kids' parents calling, she can forget about filling her stomach before the students rush back into class.

CALLER UNKNOWN

The smartphone blinks on the table. It could be a telemarketer, but she hasn't had a call like that since the construction started. Soon, the program will provide everything they need and there'll be no reason for cold calls or upsales anymore. Tiles have been laid down by the roads, on the buildings, even inside the school. They supposedly contain solar cells, but she's heard they also have something to do with augmented reality. Someone said they'd be lit up soon. That with a special set of glasses, you'd see holograms and hidden messages all around the city.

It's not just telemarketers that the earth has swallowed. Most people living in Belgrade have quit their jobs and are now refusing to leave their houses. Their main purpose in life is to wait for a thing called the Happiness-Program to kick into gear. Kids still go to school though, so unlike most, Luna still has a job to go to.

While it seems like the rest of the world is being ravaged by The Great Affliction, Serbia blooms and shines. Ever since the country's leaders gathered everyone together to live in the capital, offering them affordable living and jobs, the fertility rates have rebounded. Employment rates are down, but that doesn't concern the people who now run the city; all the citizens would soon share the same job. They'd be plugged into a system at the Server-Center, their brains used as server space for eight hours a day.

Not everyone wants to be a part of it, though; Luna's parents have made it clear that they think this new program and the people running it are pure evil. Though their rage against the new machine seems a bit exaggerated, Luna is hesitant to go against it. Her parents may be overly passionate, dramatic activists of the common good, but neither of them can be considered dumb or unsophisticated.

Whatever power possesses the Earth and its dying tenants, it hasn't yet touched Luna's city. Despite being immune to the mass-deaths, people do get restive when watching the news; the south's wildfires, the mass-suicides up north, the overpopulation in the inlands. America now has more guns lying on the roads than people using them.

But the restlessness was easy enough to fix; the city turned off all TV channels except for the ones run by the new government. Newspapers too. Online, browsing the forums and online magazines became a thing of the past, just like social media.

A complete lockdown.

A safe haven.

A bubble.

That's what Serbia had become.

The smartphone stops blinking on her desk. Luna leans back in the office chair, lifts her legs onto the table, and picks up a cabbage roll from the plastic container. She almost wishes her mother wasn't such an excellent cook; maybe then she'd be more motivated to finally move out and find a place of her own. Maybe then she could finally get a pet; Luna's father is deathly allergic to all animals but humans. Some days, he swears even people make his skin itch. Especially when the city rolls out new tech, installs it right outside their house in the city. On those days Luna's father turns silent, only to burst out in an hour-long rant later in the day.

Luna can relate. Trusting and caring for people is a tricky business these days. Before shutting down, social media made anonymity the norm. Most people work from home (if they work at all), never showing their faces or meeting people in public. It's too easy to become someone new every day. To put on a mask, hide your flaws. But without flaws, people seem to have become one and the same, all fitting the same profile; same taste, same outlook, same thoughts. It's impossible to stand out when everyone suddenly fits in.

Midday in downtown Belgrade and Luna feels as if she's living in a ghost town. The shops and offices have moved their business online. Electronic mailboxes, food-service stands, delivery drones, and self-driving cars. That's all Luna's seen today, on her way to the nearest 3D vending machine by the closed-down post office. She can't imagine finishing a meal—any meal—without a Tuplinke; a crispy nougat and milk chocolate bar. So she stuffs her pockets with these treats any time she can.

Just as she's about to bite into the first cabbage roll, the phone comes back to life. Blinking demandingly, it distracts Luna enough to make her sigh and put her lunch back into its box.

"Answer call," she says, and the blinking light turns into a green phone icon.

"This is Luna."

"Luna, it's Dan from the front desk."

"What's up, Dan?" she says happily. She likes Dan. Though his American ways make him stand out from the local crowd, it's not in a bad way. Dan hasn't molded into a lump of positive quotes, lifestyle choices, and catchphrases. At least not yet, he hasn't. "Forgot your lunch again? I'm not going to share mine, but I'll fetch you a Tuplinke or two, if you ask nicely."

But Dan doesn't chuckle or tease her back. Luna sits up and cocks her head, waiting, but the school's guard seems tongue-tied. "What's going on, Dan? Is everything okay?"

"You better just come downstairs," he says. "It's the police. They're here to see you."

The coding academy moved from the second floor to the third a few years back. This was about the same time that Luna walked in with her Computer Programming diploma and refused to leave the building until someone gave her a job. Teaching kids how to code after school wasn't exactly what she'd had in mind career-wise. Luna had hoped to participate in one of the government-funded projects, investigating international affairs and conspiracies. Just like the heroes in the paperback thrillers she devours late into every night.

But a job is a job. She'll get a bump up soon; they'd rather hire someone in-house when a new spot opens. It reduces the risk of moles and spies entering the premises.

"You do know how crazy you sound, right?" Dan had said the first time Luna told him about her plans to get promoted. "Those government funds are for a server space large enough to run some bullshit AR-program they invented in Scandinavia. It's a bunch of old folks fiddling with numbers and code snippets. Trust me, you're better off with the kiddos."

"That's exactly what they'd tell you to say if they were solving international conspiracies on the second floor, right under our noses. I can't even access that part of the building," Luna had said, waving Dan off.

"I can't believe I'm saying this. To anyone, especially in these days and times... but you're reading too many books, Luna."

The elevator doors open on the front lobby. Amused by her early memories of Dan, Luna walks to the front desk, where two police officers—a man and a woman dressed in dark-blue uniforms—stand right beside him.

Luna stops a few feet away. Dan's face is paper-white, and he dodges Luna's questioning gaze.

"Officers. Dan. What's going on?"

The woman in blue uniform steps closer and folds her hands. She gives Luna a half-smile, but her eyes fill with anxiety. Whatever news they're about to bring is not something Luna will want to hear.

"It's your parents, Radovan and Hana Novak," the woman says. Luna's heart takes off, racing against her chest. Breathing becomes difficult. She's gasping for air with small breaths.

"Are you okay? Do you have medicine for that?" The male officer steps closer. Dan hurries over to support Luna. He taps his fist on her upper back.

"I keep telling her to get her lungs checked. It's clearly asthma, but she's too stubborn to admit it."

Luna steps aside and waves Dan off. "Where are

they? Which hospital? What happened?"

The officers exchange a look. Then the woman clears her throat.

"There was a protest outside the Happiness-Program office in New Belgrade. Your parents were involved. It got out of hand, I'm afraid. The center's lobby was set on fire, and officers were attacked. The rioters had to be contained. Eleven people have died. Including your parents."

Gasp. Gasp. Gasp.

It's like her throat is shutting down, swollen, and too tired to cooperate. She can't tell whether it's asthma or the sudden panic attack that's strangling her. The room spins around her, and the three people with it. The front door flies open, and the students hurry in. Chins ducked, eyes drilling into screens, they're too occupied ranking each other on their smartphones to notice the officers and their teacher choking in the middle of the room.

Her legs wobble. All her limbs turn into strings of numbers, falling from their designated lines, scattering onto the lobby floor like broken code snippets.

"Luna, hey! Luna!" Dan's voice. Echoed. Muffled.

More words gush from under water, from the ocean of green numbers and letters. Luna flounders under their mass, trying to swim back to the surface. But the weight that pushes her down is too overwhelming. Luna lets go, floats instead of fighting the current. Somewhere on the shore, voices echo against the crashing waves.

"We need…"

"Can't breathe…"

"To the hospital."

The fluorescent lamps emit a blurry blue light. Her eyes stay open long enough to count the first row of lights. Three, four lamps in the ceiling. Luna lets her eyelids fall shut again. The tube in her throat paralyzes her. She's lying on a hard surface. Something hard presses her temples, surrounds her aching head. Then her brain detects the hurt. The excruciating pain. Her eyes fly open, staring at the blue light. The tube stops her from screaming; only a groaning sound escapes her painfully throbbing throat.

"Shit… Arnie, call Laura Solomon. City of Finland."

CALL INITIATED

"Nurse, twenty milligrams of Prodazitine and forty milligrams of Thihexamine. Keep it coming. She wasn't supposed to wake up for another thirty minutes. That's what the anesthesiologist said before he left."

"Doctor, your AR-glasses. Doctor Solomon is on the line."

Her body numb and mind blurry, all Luna can do is blink. Dreadful seconds crawl by before the pain at the back of Luna's head turns into a nagging tic, like water dripping against her skull, drilling a hole from the crown of her head to her jaw. She fights the heaviness that is her eyelids—failing. She watches the blurry images of flickering blue tubes dance around like lightsabers before they all melt into gray, then a black puddle of nothingness.

The humming sound encircles her. It echoes from wall to wall, so close to Luna's ears that she feels as if she's in the middle of the soundtrack to an online ping-pong game.

Eyelids slightly parted, she gazes into a soft purple light. Glass towers rise all around her, like a cityscape designed by architects who favor see-through building blocks over bricks, plastics, and concrete. Or is it an aquarium? Is she drowning—the humming being a filter system and the glow around her a heat lamp? Is the burning sensation deep in her throat water, penetrating her lungs, turning her into fish food?

A wiggle of toes. Fingers hovering. A slight head turn. Luna forces her body and brain to communicate with one another. The aquarium she's in is like a coffin, standing upright in a dimly lit room of endless casket rows. The door's been left open. Whatever's happening to her, whoever's doing it—they haven't yet finished.

With both hands, Luna grabs ahold of whatever is creating pressure around her skull. The helmet has wires on it, and it doesn't come off easily. Something's stuck, attached to the back of her head. Panicking, she pulls as hard as she can. Two clicks, and the helmet comes off.

She feels something wet dripping against the back of her neck. The piercing pain hits her with a delay. Grunting, she tries her best to ignore it.

One leg at a time, she climbs out of her enclosure. Left foot. Right foot. Onto a concrete stand surrounded by purple tiles, identical to the ones that snake around the New Belgrade area of the city. The kind her parents had resisted and fought against so fiercely that it cost them their lives.

When Luna steps down from the stand, a purple light gleams underneath her bare feet. She flinches back from a sudden sharp pain that causes her to lose her balance and stumble. Naked and alone, she sits in the head-piercing light. Where are her clothes? Why is she here and not at the Coding Academy, teaching and eating cabbage rolls? Where is "here"?

She forces herself up. Supporting herself against a metal cart lined with a neat array of tools, Luna slips and knocks a tablet to the floor. The device lights up, revealing a chart and a picture; Luna's face.

Ignoring the pain, she picks up the pad and waits for her blurred vision to focus. Then she reads.

Luna Novak. Twenty-three-year-old programmer.

Parents deceased in an anti-chip riot.

Patient chipping failed due to early awakening mid-operation.

Unchipped test subject. Medically induced coma.

To be stored in stasis 736662. City of Serbia.

The more she reads, the clearer her head becomes.

Holding onto the pad like it's a map to safety, Luna looks around in the enormous dimly lit space. Is it a storage facility? No, not enough windows. An industrial warehouse of some sort?

She walks to the closest stasis capsule. Unlike hers, this one's door is not open. She presses her forehead against the tinted glass to get a better look inside.

A naval.

Body hair.

Nipples.

The sleeping face of a middle-aged man.

In terror, Luna pulls back and drops the tablet onto the floor. The purple light turns to a gray glimmer. Panic washes through her, then a rush of adrenaline. Spinning around like a drunk ballerina, she looks for a door. Or a hatch. Stairs. Anything to get her out of this hole.

The purple tiles light up under her feet. Adrenaline makes the pain at the back of her head easier to bear. She counts five capsules, then ten, then fifteen, as she makes her way down an aisle. She starts to run.

More capsules appear; the rows are endless. Out of breath from running, Luna stops near three gurneys and a storage box of some sort. She kneels down and tries to open the box, but a small pad with a lock icon on its screen stops her from accessing whatever is inside. Luna gets up, pulls a white sheet from one of the gurneys, and wraps it around her naked body.

Then she runs.

After fifty or more stasis capsules, another open area appears. Shelves and drawers. Lab shoes and coveralls. Luna reaches for a pair; rough purple fabric with a long zipper on the front. It must be three sizes too large. Rummaging through the pile of fabrics, she can't find anything that would fit her better. She pulls the coveralls on over the sheet, folding the overly-long arm and leg sleeves, and continues to rummage through the storage area. It's mostly medicine bottles and boxes. First aid supplies, water bottles, dead smartphones and electrical pads identical to the ones she saw earlier. Shoes, gloves, face masks, and canned goods.

One of the drawers is filled with purple fabric bags. Luna picks one out and starts shoving random objects inside; duct tape, batteries, candles, flashlight, a hand mirror, a notebook and pens, three cans of vegetable and noodle soup, and a water bottle. Do these things belong to the unconscious people in the tubes?

She opens a bottle of water and gulps it down. Her throat burns, and her stomach twitches, but the water stays down, rummaging around in her empty stomach. There's no time to eat, not even if it's her last meal. She needs to at least try and escape this nightmare.

She takes off running again.

But her body's too tormented. Her mind wrenched after her sudden adrenaline spike. She slows to a walk, then bends over and collapses on the tile floor. The purple glimmer forces her eyes shut, and she holds her head between her hands.

"Keep running, sweetheart. Keep going."

The voice booms from somewhere near. Very near. Between-her-ears-near. Luna presses her palms on her temples and moans.

"You can do this. Just thirty more capsules."

The voice belongs to a woman speaking in her native Serbian. It must be someone from her past, but Luna can't recognize who speaks the calm, well-pronounced words.

"Am I dead? Are you here to pick me up?" she asks.

"You're very much alive. And before you ask, no, you're not going insane. But you must hurry, or they'll find you. Keep going."

She stumbles forward on all fours. The oversized coveralls make her slip on the tiles, so she gets to her feet. She should have picked a pair of lab shoes. Too late now. Her head throbbing in agony, she jogs forward.

After what seems like hours of forcing her feet to cooperate with her racing mind, Luna sees a shadow ahead. A wall. With stairs. One of the pant sleeves unrolls and, tripping on it, she crumples back onto the floor. Crawling toward the stairs, Luna starts to weep.

"You're doing great, sweetheart. Just a bit more to go."

One step at a time, she drags her partly numb body up the purple stairs. Halfway up, she stops to listen. People talking, somewhere above her.

The door handle feels hot in her hand. The purple light has become intolerable to look at. Luna closes her eyes and presses her ear against the metal door. Muffled chattering and laughter reach her ears from a few feet away. She waits for the people to move, for the ripple of conversation to end. But new voices appear, some now closer to the door that is Luna's only hope for escape.

She slides down to sit. The tile stairs feel hard against her backside. Luna reaches for the escaping pant sleeve, wraps it back up. From the fabric bag, she fishes out the hand mirror and a flashlight. In the narrow light beam, she investigates her face in the mirror's reflection. A pale and tired face stares back at her, eyes wide and rounded with terror.

She needs to walk out. Pretend she belongs here. That she's one of the people who wear the purple coveralls, stashing naked people into scary-looking storage tubes. Like in one of her paperbacks; she'll need to outsmart those who have captured her.

Scratching an itch at the back of her head, her hand touches something wet. She winces under the touch. The flashlight reveals a bloody hand; the back of her skull is still bleeding. The fabric against her back is drenched. Before she has time to think about it, Luna wipes her wet hand on the front of her coveralls. A hand-shaped blood stain now decorates her stolen outfit.

"That was stupid," she whispers to herself. "Like you need to draw more attention to yourself."

What's done is done. Luna holds the purple bag in front of the stain. She does her best to cover the bald patch on her head with whatever hair her kidnappers have left her with. She cracks the door open and sticks the hand mirror out to see a reflection of the people outside.

They stand in three groups, men and women in purple and purple-green coveralls. Chitchatting, they sip from metal travel cups. Some of them are wearing blinking, odd-looking sunglasses.

Luna slips through the door and stands next to a plastic Yucca palm tree. She closes her fists around the bag to stop her hands from shaking. Her coverall grows heavy and sticks to her skin. She feels lightheaded.

She scans the open space, looking for a way out. Stadium-sized screens shine purple, but Luna can't see anything on them. Still, some of the people with sunglasses stare at them, or point at them while nodding.

The tall building has corridors with see-through railings. Five floors above, a glass ceiling reveals a sunny day. On the roof of an over-street corridor connecting two buildings, bird droppings decorate the glass surface.

At the end of the first floor—the one with Luna and a Yucca palm tree—revolving doors spin as purple coveralls enter and exit the building.

"That's the only way out," the woman in her head says. *"Don't look around. Don't stop for anything. Just keep your chin up and go."*

Luna does as the voice tells her to do. Her bare feet make a faint flapping sound on the floor tiles. The people with glasses don't see her passing by, but the ones without glasses turn to stare at her. Two men whisper to one another, nodding toward Luna. One of them clears his throat.

"Excuse me, Miss?"

Luna keeps going.

"Miss, can I see your CS-card?"

The pant sleeve unwraps itself again. Luna stumbles on it, falls hard on her knees.

"Holy chip. Miss, what happened to your shoes? Is that blood on your uniform?"

Luna scrambles to her feet and takes off running, eyes fixated on the revolving door.

"Hey! Stop that girl!"

The pant sleeve flapping along, Luna runs faster and faster. Footsteps echo behind her, but she doesn't turn to look over her shoulder. She gets to the doors, slips through, and blunders out the other end. Three people—the two men without glasses and one with them—bounce into one another, all trying to ram into the doorway at the same time.

Luna takes a right and keeps on running. She leaps into a large waterfall fountain, sloshes her way across it to get to an alley next to the building she's just escaped from. There she strips off her water and blood-soaked coveralls and continues with only a sheet wrapped around her. Without the oversized attire slowing her down, she makes it to the corner and takes a left turn before the men have reached the alleyway.

No footsteps follow her into the park. No shouts split

the air as she continues her escape through New Belgrade, onto the old main street, and to the suburbs where she grew up. A strange feeling of homesickness comes over her, but how can she feel that way? She's jogging down her home street now. At the end of the road, she rushes through the front gate, knocking it off its hinges. She turns over the decorative rocks by the back door until—instead of worms and beetles—she finds the spare key. She rushes inside and closes the door.

There's more blood now; parts of the white sheet are glued onto her back. She folds herself in half, sits down on the living room floor. A ten-hour nap. That's what she needs. But will it be safe here?

"It's not safe. They know where you live. Where your parents lived."

Unsure whether she feels foolish or insane, Luna answers the voice that booms inside her injured head. "What should I do then? Where do I go?"

"Patch your head. Pack all the medicine you can find. Put on some clothes that you'd wear on a camping trip to the woods. Then go."

"Go where?"

"To the woods. We'll find you."

"But this is my home. I don't have anyone left, there's no one to take care of me."

"Only you can take care of you. In the end, no one else will have your back. And sweetheart, if anything is the end then this is it."

Most of the log house has collapsed. Only two walls hold the roof off the ground. Moss and weeds surround the abandoned building's rock and brick base. Inside, it seems almost cozy. The long dark-green drapes and the old fireplace remind Luna of winter nights in her childhood, when her father would read the family old Slavic tales from one of the storybooks.

Then the sun goes down.

The wind blows across the ruins, waving the ripped curtains around. The loose floorboards creak under Luna's weight as she tries to get more comfortable. Head hurting and her throat too raspy for speaking, she hugs her legs and rocks back and forth. What does it matter if she becomes mute now? She has no one to talk to. No one who'll tell her a comforting bedtime story of some magical creature that lives in the woods, playing guitar, destroying evil witches.

What is she to eat? Cold soup, straight from the can? That will have to do. She hasn't cooked a meal in her life. And her mother's mouthwatering cooking has turned her into someone who wouldn't touch junk food if her life depended on it… which it now does.

The long grass rustles behind the wall, snapping Luna out of her dark thoughts, bringing her into her even darker reality. Holding her breath, she listens. More rustling. Sniffing. A shadow glides by in the darkness. Then another.

An evil witch? *Babaroga*?

The snout pokes from the corner. In the dim

moonlight, Luna can only see a bit of dark hair around it. But it's definitely a snout. Not a witch's wart-covered nose.

Yes, because that's so much better, she thinks. *Being eaten alive by a pack of wolves.*

More footsteps behind the wall. Another snout appears. Then a head, a canine body. Then a third one. A yellow mutt, a brown pit bull, and a black sheep dog with knotted fur jump up on the log house's floor. Two of them stare at Luna, the third sniffs around the boards, carrying something in its mouth.

Babaroga's hand? A leg?

Then the yellow wandering dog comes toward Luna, sitting in the corner, pressed against the log wall. It drops something on the floor and nudges it toward her. The tennis ball rolls across the tilted floor, stops in front of Luna's hiking boot. The dogs all wag their tails. The yellow mutt barks once.

"Seriously? I die and come back to life, and you want to *play ball?*"

Another bark.

She picks up the tennis ball and throws it across the room. The dogs rush after it, bring it back in a matter of seconds. Luna throws again. And again. And again.

They play until Luna's on the verge of falling asleep. She's not cold, not in the layers of hiking clothes she's wearing, found untouched in her closet. But she is hungry. Thirsty. And whether it's the raspy throat or the wheezing breath, it's getting harder and harder to breathe.

"Here, boy. You want to lie down with me? I need to close my eyes. But just for a moment."

The yellow dog hurries over to Luna, lies down next to her. The two other dogs, the tiny one and the black one, sit side by side at the edge of the crumbling ruins. Are they standing guard?

"We'll figure this out tomorrow..." she mumbles, already fast asleep.

The dogs hear the footsteps approaching first. Luna tries to focus on the steps, to figure out whether the three dogs are part of a bigger pack. Then she hears the voice. The same woman that helped her escape the stasis capsule and the basement.

"Over there, in the corner." The woman's voice is low and smooth. "Go on, pick her up. She can't weigh more than fifty kilos."

"She's covered with blood. She'll make a mess."

"I'll make a mess of you, if—"

"Okay, okay. I'm on it."

When the man's boots come closer, the yellow mutt growls.

"Easy, boy," Luna murmurs, still half asleep. "Easy."

"Sloboda, we're not bringing the dog."

"The dogs," the woman corrects him.

"Sloboda, please."

The woman doesn't reply.

"Oh, the hell with it..."

When he lifts her limp form, Luna wraps her arms around the dog, holds him tight against her body.

Floating, swinging, her head against a stranger's shoulder, she lets him carry her and her new best friend home.

CHAPTER 4
PURPLE CITY

The pills are shaped like American footballs. They rest against her palm, together with smaller tablets: painkillers. Five people stand around Luna in an office that is supposedly hers now. The walk through the purple city and into the Chip-Center has given her a raging headache.

"My apologies," Iris had said, walking in front of her, leading the way. "I should have brought the pills with me. I guess I'm not used to bringing Unchipped into the city."

Luna scoffed but followed Iris toward a building she had once run away from, covered with a white hospital sheet and oversized uniform. "You mean, you're not used to bringing my kind in while we're *conscious*?"

"Huh," Iris had said. "I guess it has been a while."

Now in the office, on the gray side of the building, where the lamps and machines emit a warm yellow light instead of the piercing neon-purple preferred by the

Chipped, Luna is dying to take those pills. The painkillers, at least, not the other ones. Most likely, she'll end up back in the basement, but playing along might buy her enough time to make sure Marić is alive and breathing. She'd better play along.

"Here," Iris says. "Have some water."

One of the soldiers dressed in purple and green coveralls brings over a plastic bottle of water. After checking that it's sealed—not that the Chipped wouldn't be crafty enough to stage an untouched drink—Luna picks out the pain killers, tosses them into her mouth, and washes them down with the water.

One of the older soldiers clears her throat. "I highly recommend that you—"

"Yeah, well, I'm not known to take suggestions from people who killed my parents and trapped me in an underground hellhole."

"But one of the computers you'll be working with is a CS-key," she continues. Iris shakes her head a bit, gesturing for her colleague to stop talking.

"Am I supposed to know what that means?" Luna says. She rolls the cap onto the water bottle, bangs it against the empty white plastic table.

"The CS-keys are just old-fashioned computers turned into a lock-key system which integrates with your handprint. But the rebels use them as computers. Kaarina's believed to have one. And that's why we use them this way too."

"Even if we have more advanced computers at hand?"

"This one is both. See?" Iris points at the blinking purple light. "Two birds and however that old saying goes."

"But the lights hurt my—"

"If you're to find a rebel, you need to think as one."

Luna considers this. "I don't know, sounds kinda dumb to me."

Iris scratches her blue-white head, then waves her hand. The soldiers leave the room, some of them shrugging, some clearly relieved to leave this smelly, uncooperative creature alone with Iris. The door shuts behind them. The only sound is the ventilation system, blowing fresh air into the room.

Iris nudges the pills closer to Luna.

"I'm not taking these pills," Luna says, shaking her head. "I don't care if my life depends on it."

"And how do you know those aren't the painkillers? The tablets you already took could have been the blockers..."

She stares at Iris' amused face. Blockers? That's what they're called? And has Iris tricked her into taking them? Will Luna collapse now and be taken back to the stasis capsule with her name on it downstairs in the basement?

Iris laughs a little, then walks across the room to open a cabinet in the wall. "You should feel better in a few minutes. The painkillers are eight-hundred milligrams."

Luna sets the remaining pills on the desk and folds her arms. This isn't starting out too well. The last time she was in this building, Iris's kind damn near turned her into rutabaga. And all this woman can do is make threats and push her buttons. Agitated, tempted to walk out the door and see how far she can run this time, Luna sits on the desk and waits. From the closet, Iris fishes out a tablet, a keyboard, a mouse, an old-fashioned laptop, a set of AR-glasses, and a metal object that looks like a bracelet.

"The CS-key will get you into the chip-net. The laptop is for backup, database views, and note-keeping. What else do you need to start working? Don't tell me you still use pen and paper?"

"Got any chocolate bars around here?"

Iris looks up from the pile of technology she's spread out across the table. She investigates Luna's face for a few seconds, maybe trying to read her thoughts, maybe figuring out if she's serious.

"We've got some raw chocolate in the break room. Vegan-bars too. You're welcome to anything you can find."

Luna nods, her eyes locked on the CS-key. Iris taps a code in, then checks some boxes, and flips the thing over on the desk. She slides it over to where Luna is sitting. "Place your hand in the middle of the screen. That'll give you access and keep others out."

"No one else can access it? Not even you?"

"Ha. You should be so lucky."

She follows Iris's instructions. After her handprint appears on the pad's screen, a green light begins blinking on it. Luna winces and looks away. Maybe she should take the blocker thingies, whatever evil crap they are. Working with this technology isn't just painful; it makes her confused and slow. Tired.

"And what's that bracelet thing?"

"I'm glad you asked." Iris takes the round metal ring, walks over to Luna's side of the table. "Kick off one shoe and lift up your pant leg." Her shoe lands on the floor beside the desk. Luna reaches for her ankle and wraps the trousers up, showing her bare calf. The metal bracelet has small hinges. It opens in half. Iris clicks it around Luna's ankle.

"There. Now you can go feed those beasts of yours at night. You can even sleep at the farm if that's what you want. Just be here at eight a.m. every morning."

"What, no days off?"

Iris walks to the office door, opens it to walk out. "Not until you find the rebels."

Her job is to hack into old security cameras across the City of Finland and the City of England. On the laptop, Luna has four headshots pulled up on the screen.

A girl with short blonde hair and a scar across the side of her face.

A guy with overgrown hair, AR-glasses, and a kind smile.

Another guy, scars and bruises scattered around his strong jaw and stern face.

And a third man, this one with long dreadlocks tied up into a knot, his skin many shades darker than the rest of the rebels.

Unchipped Kaarina #6529F

Chipped Markus #75294F

Unchipped *Unknown* #0000F

Unchipped William #9461C

These are the underdogs that Luna is supposed to hunt down. Why—she's not sure. But she knows where they'll end up if she finds them–in a basement somewhere. The only thing she doesn't know is which city will provide their final resting place.

"None of your business, Luna..." she mumbles to herself. A green light flashes on the CS-key. Another security camera, a new crowd of people.

Luna leans closer to the screen, ignoring the pressure in her skull. Two women and a man. The City of England, sixteen days ago. They're wearing proper red coveralls, looking like most Chipped people do. But they're way too far from downtown, close enough to the city limits that the guards would surely turn them around, if they happened to pass by. One of them holds a piece of paper, with letters on it. Luna zooms closer, but can only read part of the leaflet's heading.

CFU

Something fishy's going on.

"Come on, come on... Turn around. Let me see your pretty little faces."

The man turns to face the camera. He looks around

to scan the premises; an old warehouse with debris and junk spread all over the asphalt yard. Coal-dark hair. Big round nose. Lopsided glasses—the old-fashioned kind. He looks nothing like the photos on the laptop screen.

Then, something moves outside the broken-down fence that the trio is standing near. They all kneel down, taking off their oversized backpacks. The screen freezes, and Luna zoom closer. The closer she gets to the face on the camera, the blurrier it gets.

"Go figure."

She pushes play and lets the recording roll. All three bags disappear through the hole in the fence, grabbed by whoever is on the other side. Then the potato nose and his companions get up, scan the premises one more time, and scatter in three different directions.

Luna taps fast-forward.

Plastic bags twirling in the wind. That's all that remains.

The knock on the office door startles Luna. She's been staring into the security camera's live feeds for—how long? Two hours? Four? She looks up and sees Iris, staring at her from the doorway.

"Did you find something, or why are you still here? Your shift ends at five. It's eight o'clock."

"I just found a few more cameras to check. Which reminds me..." she says, her gaze still attached on the screen. "Why are we going through old security feed? I mean, don't you have someone watching this all day long?"

"Hardly. There are no break-ins in the city. No crime. Well, except for the old stores, those are looted from time to time, but who cares. We have a guard checking the facilities once a day, and that's plenty."

"Just one guard?"

Iris shrugs a shoulder.

"Okay… but either way. I still don't understand why you need *me* to do this. This is quite far from actual programming work. Anyone could do this."

Iris walks in. "And yet, here you are."

What is that supposed to mean? Luna opens her mouth to ask but then changes her mind. She rests her elbows on the desk and buries her head in her hands. When Iris walks over to her, she doesn't bother to look up. Three pills and a water bottle appear on the table, right under her nose.

"I think that's enough for today," Iris says. "Would you like to stay here for the night? We have rooms for your kind. It's not much, but there's no AR-stuff in there. Completely safe for the Unchipped."

"What luxury."

"We like to keep our guests happy."

Luna leans back, throws the pills into her mouth, and washes them down with water. "Any vacancy downstairs? In the basement?"

"Why, you're missing your old capsule?"

"Just curious. Last I visited, there were more

prisoners down there than people living in this city. What is their purpose anyway?"

Iris tilts her head, stares at Luna with a partly amused, and partly disinterested look on her face. It's clear she has no intention of educating Luna on city politics. Then her chest pocket starts blinking, and a soft vibrating sound breaks the uncomfortable silence in the room. Or maybe it's only uncomfortable for Luna; nothing seems to bother her new blue-haired boss.

She picks up the AR-glasses, puts them on. "Yeah? No, still here. Yeah, the bracelet's on. Mm." Iris walks to the doorway, then turns to look at Luna. She lifts them so she can see better. "You're going home then? To the farm?"

"Of course I'm going home. That was the deal, right? I get to stay with the dogs?"

A shrug. The glasses fall back on Iris's face. "Suit yourself. Just be careful when you get up. First days can be tough for a damaged mind like yours."

"I'll show you brain damage, you piece of..." Luna mumbles, but Iris is already gone.

The light in the corridor shifts from warm, soft yellow to acid purple as she makes her way toward the Chip-Center's front lobby. Dizzy and nauseated, Luna has to stop frequently to lean against a wall and rest. As much as she hates to admit it, Iris was right. The CS-key has pulled a trick on her brain—painkillers or no painkillers.

Maybe Marić can tell her what the blockers do? Iris swears they'll take care of the pain that the AR-technology causes her, but why would Luna ever believe anything a Chipped person says? They might even turn her into a mindless robot. Does Marić take the pills himself?

Continuing through the lobby, Luna squints to avoid the purple glow ahead of her. The whole building is silent.

Ahead, the revolving door rotates. A man steps in carrying a long black duffel bag. Guns? Empty body bags? Luna lowers her gaze but keeps her eyes open. Who cares what these monsters do after office hours?

She's almost out. Chin against her chest, she passes the man with the suspicious bag.

"Hey, do I know you?"

Luna doesn't slow down, ignoring the man. But by the revolving door, he catches up to Luna and blocks her way out.

"It *is* you," he says. "Bloody-Mary!"

Luna looks up, tries to give a polite smile but fails miserably. "Jovan. Good to see you. Now could you kindly get the hell out of my way so I can leave this torture chamber?"

"That's right, the lights! They're obnoxious for you. They interfere with your peripheral nervous system. Am I right?"

You're obnoxious to me, Luna thinks, but doesn't say it out loud. "Big words for someone who measures land for a living." She side-steps and clears her throat, nodding at the revolving door. "You know, if you're trying to be my friend, capitalizing on the unequal power dynamic between us is not the way to go. And this is the second time you've done something like this."

"Oh, shit! Sorry." Jovan steps aside. "That really was not my intention. I was just happy to see—"

Luna stops listening to his explanations. She hurries out the door. But outside, the purple buildings' glow is like a baseball bat against her face. She stumbles backward, bumps into the spinning door, and falls to the ground, right onto the tile road.

"Shit, are you okay?" Jovan is by her side in a few seconds, lifting her off the warm purple panels. Are they heated? In this weather?

"Did you hit your head?" Jovan asks, dusting off invisible dirt from Luna's back. The tiles look like they get cleaned with toothbrushes and elbow grease after anyone walks on them.

"Stop groping me," Luna says. She takes a step back, pulls her inhaler from her pocket. She takes a puff and stands—her eyes closed, and her back turned to Jovan. Maybe he'll be smart enough to take the hint. To leave her be.

"Groping?" he says, eyes wide and filled with shock. "I would never... Hey don't they have that medicine? For your kind? Kind of an antidote, what's it called..."

Luna sighs and shoves the inhaler back into her pocket. She starts to walk toward the waterfall fountain.

She'll need to talk to Marić about those damn blockers.

"Hey, wait! What's your rush, Mary?" Jovan yells after her.

Luna stops but doesn't turn around to look at him. She despises him, but she's still at his mercy. He could report her. She could end up dead. Marić too. They both probably will, now that she thinks about it. What purpose do two Unchipped people have in the city? When one is as good as a binge-drinking drunk in a local pub and the other collapses in front of the office after a single day's work?

Shaking her head, she walks on. Fuck it. What difference does it make? What he thinks of her, what Luna thinks of him... it'll never matter. What an Unchipped thinks—in the city or outside of it—is irrelevant.

Back at the farmhouse, the dogs raise a ruckus. They jump against the broken gate, tails wagging, paws rattling the rickety fencing. Luna waits for Marić to yell at them from the main house, but even if he did so, Luna wouldn't be able to hear him over the excited whining and grunting. She checks the main house windows; none of the lights are on. Marić is not home. Is he working late in the city?

"Okay, okay. Can you let me in? It's hard to feed you guys if you crush me alive before I get to the pantry."

As if they understand each word, the dogs let Luna pass among them, splitting into two jumping and wiggling rows of happy faces. Through the open sliding doors, Luna walks in and heads straight to the pantry closet. Two plastic scoops filled with dog chow, she walks around the room and leaves piles of kibble on the floor. Then she fills the scoops and makes a round of refills. The plastic bowls would be too much work. They'll be fine eating off the floor for one night.

She crashes onto the mattress. The Christmas tree lights bounce at the impact of her weight landing on the bed, throwing waves of shadows around the room. Walking from the city took enough time to clear her head and get rid of her nausea, but it also cost the rest of her strength. The day's been long. All she wants is to go to bed, but she needs to talk to Marić first. Not just about the blockers, but everything that's happened over the last twenty-four hours.

"Where the hell are you..." she mumbles, fighting her heavy eyelids. Wacko and the new dog jump on the mattress. They lie down; two bundles of sighs and contented grunts, the yellow mutt next to Luna's head, and the limping dog by her legs. Luna gives in to the fatigue and closes her eyes. *Just for a moment*, she thinks, *and then I'll get up and find the Reverend.*

The piercing pain sends her flying up off the mattress. She dances around the room, jumping on one foot and holding her ankle with her hands. The bracelet around her ankle shines with a bright purple light, making it impossible for her to look at it.

"You sons of bitches, turn this thing off!" she yells, unsure who it is she's yelling at. The Chipped are miles away.

"Marić..."

She lets go of her leg, limps to the open door with a crack in its frame. In the main house, the kitchen is clean; no coffee mugs or empty moonshine bottles clutter the counters or the table.

"Marić? I need you!" she yells, folding in half. The tremendous pain around her ankle has turned into burning agony. Could this thing cut her foot off? It sure feels like it. She makes her way to the hallway, knocks on Marić's bedroom door.

"Marić, you've got to wake up," she says, stumbling on her own feet. "Help me...agghh," she bites her lip in agony, "Help me get this thing off."

No answer. The house is as quiet as it was the day Sloboda took her last breath and left Marić gasping for air and willingness to live. Luna opens the bedroom door; no one's in. The bed is made, which is out of character for the Reverend. Another thing that reminds her of Sloboda.

The pain is turning her ankle numb. She limps back into the kitchen and finds Wacko pawing the fridge. Luna opens the door and looks in; several days worth of food, fresh bottles of moonshine, dairy goods. There's no way Marić would have left this for her and the dogs to eat.

The bracelet begins to vibrate, somehow linking with Luna's head, making her bend over in torment. Wacko licks her face, making a high-pitched whine. She lies down on the kitchen floor, crawls into a fetal position.

"Make it stop, make it stop, make it stop..."

The pressure in her head grows more demanding. It's like a relentless knocking against her temples. A knife pressing into her forehead. A drill entering the back of her skull. Luna buries her head in her arms, rocks herself on the floor. More dogs run in, surrounding their master in distress. Luna holds on to Tiny, pressing her against her chest.

The wheezing of her breath mixes with the whining of her companions. Even Wacko has stopped investigating the open fridge. He tilts his yellow head. With every wheezing breath she draws, he cocks his head to the other side. Then he runs off. Books thump against the floor at Luna's side of the house. Dishes clink as the dog rummages around the mattress. Then Wacko's snout is back, shoving something hard against Luna's buried face; her inhaler.

She takes a puff, holds it in, then exhales anxiety and a whiff of death. Still on the floor with dogs sitting around her, some pressing gently against her side, back, and chest, she lets go of the agony and breathes deeply. She tries to ignore the pain around her ankle, the panic of Marić disappearing, the agony in her head. Another deep breath. Then another.

"Lu? What the hell are you doing?"

The voice echoes inside her numb brain.

"Why the hell is my fridge door open? I have real yogurt in there for heaven's sake."

Luna focuses on her breath, doesn't answer. As she closes her eyes, images of a dimly lit room with no windows flicker on her closed eyelids. A woman with arms folded against her chest leans against the door. Iris. Staring at Luna. No—staring at Marić. She's seeing through Marić's eyes, not her own. She's forgotten that tapping another Unchipped let you exist in two places at once.

She brings the inhaler to her lips, takes another puff.

"She's at the farmhouse. Lying on my kitchen floor. Told you she didn't try to escape, Iris. She just forgot to set her alarm."

"It's out of batteries," Luna breathes out. "Marić, I'm in a lot of pain. Is she trying to kill me?"

"Iris, please. Turn off the bracelet. Send a car. Luna will come willingly, I promise."

Through her landlord's eyes, Luna stares at the woman with blue-white hair. A metal toothpick stuck between her teeth, Iris stares at him silently. After what seems like an agonizing eternity, she then pulls out her AR-glasses from the chest pocket of her coveralls and brings them to her lips. With a low voice, she says a command to her microphone.

The pain around Luna's ankle subsides. A breath of relief escapes her lips, just before she vomits on the floor.

"Tell her to be here in half an hour," Iris says before she leaves the room. A metal door whooshes shut and locks with a click.

"What the hell was that?" Luna says, her voice unnaturally high. The dogs cock their heads, still staring.

Marić slides down to sit on a gray tiled floor. He folds his hands as if he's about to pray. But Luna knows his faith is just a façade. Part of his work with the Chipped. "You know how you're always five days late with the rent, Lu?"

She sits up on the floor, supported by Wacko sitting next to her. "Really? That's what you want to talk about? Late fees?"

"Just answer the question."

"Yes, I'm well aware. I'm a lousy tenant. A terrible person."

"Well, Lu. This is you being late for work. Much like unpaid rent, though your so-called landlord in the city is not quite as forgiving as I am."

"They thought I fled? And what is this wormhole they're keeping you in? Is this your office?"

"Does this look like an office? No, Lu. I'm in one of the cell units in the Chip-Center. And if you ever want to see daylight again, I suggest you stop rolling in dog hair and self-pity and get your late ass back to the city."

Luna gets up from the floor. "You're a prisoner?"

"Looks like."

"When are they letting you out?"

The Reverend spreads his hands, then folds them again. "That's up to you, kiddo. Better get cracking."

With her T-shirt on backward and still wearing pajama bottoms, Luna parks Sloboda's old bike by the Chip-Center's front door. There's no need to lock it; the Chipped all have self-driving vehicles to get around with. Only Marić uses a bike to commute.

She walks through the revolving doors and into the hallway. The people are all wearing AR-glasses, which makes Luna practically invisible to them. She hurries toward the back of the building, where the neon-purple AR-world changes into soft yellow illumination.

The office door is open. Iris sits by Luna's desk, a metal toothpick between her full lips. Without looking up from the CS-key screen, her voice pierces the room. "How was your beauty sleep?"

Avoiding the CS-key's purple light, Luna scans the office table for pain killers. She needs at least three to make it through this day. "Could have been better. Woke up with a headache and my foot being cut off."

"Poor baby," Iris says, her eyes still investigating the screens. The laptop's screen shows code snippets instead of headshots. "Maybe some good ol' hacking will wake you up. While you slept in, I got a hit."

"You found the rebels?"

"Sort of. I found them—but a week ago."

"Where at?"

Iris puts on her AR-glasses, taps the air, and swipes around a database that Luna has no access to—glasses or no glasses. She waits while Iris searches for something, her fingers pinching and patting until she reaches for her glasses and sets them on the table. Luna looks away, wondering if she could make a quick trip into the break room and make herself a cup of coffee.

"Margaret Lewis. City of England. No idea what they did with the over hundred kids they kidnapped from Kinship Care, but Kaarina and her crew were definitely with her. The city cameras caught them by Lewis's place of residence."

"So this Margaret is, what? A local Unchipped leader?"

"Nope."

"Was she trying to turn them in?" Luna asks. She'd need at least three servings of shitty Grab-a-Cups before she'd be able to keep up with Iris's poor communication skills.

"She let them go. Brought a pregnant girl into the hospital and disappeared into thin air. The last we saw her was when the most wanted Unchipped rebel visited her house in the suburbs."

"And no one can find her? This Margaret person?"

"Not yet. But we will. All I know is that somehow, she got her hearing back, too. Years of access to Solomon's latest cochlea and vestibular research, and she refuses the surgery. Then does it to herself. Fixing her chip in the process."

"She's Chipped? Helping rebels?"

"Look at that," Iris says, clapping her hands lazily. "You're catching up. For a brief moment, the headquarters' computer showed us her chip was activated and traceable. Then, she vanished into a thin air. Just like all the rebels did when they first disappeared from the cities. Whatever firewalls Margaret came up with to block us from tracking the chips, it's top-notch."

"And when did you realize the mole was Margaret? When her chip disappeared from the system?"

A nod. "We've been looking for the mole for months now. Someone is covering up the rebel tracks, that much we've known all along. I just didn't know it'd be someone at the top."

"The top?"

"Margaret is one of the Happiness-Program founders. She's also our best programmer."

"That must have pissed you off so bad."

Iris looks at Luna with a frown on her face, waiting for her to elaborate.

"Not being able to put her away by now. Isn't that what you do? Store the misfits in capsules and use their brains for God knows what?"

"Funny. You mentioning God," Iris says, a half-smile wiping away her frown. "Is the Reverend's work growing on you? Do you really believe in such things?"

The room is spinning. Luna sidesteps farther away from the purple light and the screens. "Speaking of which… why are you keeping Marić in a cell somewhere? Why is he in trouble? And now that you've found the mole and located the rebels, isn't my job here over?"

"Quite the opposite."

Iris gets up and circles the table. Luna hopes she'll dig out a pill bottle or give her something for the pain. Anything. She's almost ready to ask for the blockers—whatever it takes to bring her head back into this time and space.

"I need you to hack into Margaret's computer. She's still somewhere, and she's going to make a mistake at some point. If she hasn't already."

"You want me to hack *her*? The Chipped's best programmer?"

"One of the best. No one is irreplaceable. And let's keep this between us for now. The fewer people who know about Margaret the better. Until we find her, I mean."

"You don't need to report this to the headquarters?"

"That's the last thing we need: me, AR-calling one of the founders. Who knows what software Lewis has installed and where. No, we must trace her whereabouts, everything since that day when Kaarina was at her house. I don't care how many hours it takes. Find a gap. Get in. Report to me and me alone."

"I'll need more painkillers."

"All I have is blockers."

"And what do they do? Does Marić take them?"

"Of course not. If he did, he'd be useless to us. Even more so than he is now."

"I don't understand."

"You're not here to understand. Or to ask questions." Iris walks by her, bumping Luna's shoulder on the way by. The impact makes her head throb.

"There's a medical box in the break room. Maybe if you're lucky, someone with a working brain will open it up for you." She turns on her heels, blue hair dancing around her unnaturally beautiful face. "And hey," Iris says, reaching for the metal toothpick between her lips. "Next time you're late for work, I'll turn your reverend friend into dog chow."

The break room is full of purple overalls, sitting with AR-glasses on, staring into a reality that doesn't interest Luna one bit. Will she be forced to join them after this rebel hunt is done and dealt with? Or will they simply kill her, or worse—stuff her into a capsule where she'll spend the rest of her days braindead and forgotten?

The medical box is located next to a 3D printer, installed on the back wall of the room. A narrow rim of purple light shines from its edges. There's no way she could get it open, even if it didn't have some Chipped technology keeping it locked away from outsiders.

Luna clears her throat and spreads her arms, waving

to the room. They all keep still, staring off into space. "Hey, umm. Fellas?"

No one moves an inch.

"Care to help a friend out?"

Would these people remember what that means—a friend? And who is Luna to call them that? They've never met before. They're hardly meeting now.

One of the purple coveralls takes off his glasses.

Shit.

"Hey, Bloody-Mary! Sorry, I missed it. What do you need?"

Of course it's Jovan. From a crowd of twenty people.

"Do those things make you deaf too? I thought you could still see and hear the real world through the glasses."

Jovan walks over to her and gives her a smile. "You say the real world, we say the past. This is how we communicate now. Message boards, trailer videos, and databases. The glasses anticipate all your wants and needs so effectively that it's almost like they read your mind." Jovan looks up as if to consider something. "I guess to an outsider, we may seem a bit strange."

"You say strange. I say brainless sheep."

Jovan laughs and spreads his hands. A friendly gesture. She'd be pleasantly surprised—if it didn't come from the person who put her in this mess in the first place. Jovan was surely the one who told Iris about Luna.

"Do you work here now, or what? Are you scheduled for re-chipping?"

"That's none of your business."

Jovan lifts his hands and shows his palms. "Fair enough. I'm known for asking too many questions. But I also respect people's privacy."

"Clearly."

"Hey, no need to get your glasses in a glitch. I'm just glad you're here. It's not safe out there right now. And I know being here is not exactly what you wanted, but if you ever want to talk about..."

When Luna feels her face flushing, she turns and walks away. Jovan doesn't follow her. No one does.

Fool me once, shame on the Chipped. Fool me twice... no. She'll never trust anyone in this building. Or ask for their help. She'll wing it—go through her day without pills.

What's the worst that could happen?

Sweat drips from her forehead and onto the desk. Luna pinches the bridge of her nose, but there's nothing she can do to diminish the headache. The laptop in front of her displays green numbers and letters. Though the CS-key that Iris has provided Luna with is ten times faster and more efficient than any of the other devices she uses, she had to put it in a drawer. But the effect the purple light has on her hasn't gone away. The device being out of sight has hardly lessened the agony it brings.

All her brute force attacks have bounced back. She's found the right device—Margaret's work computer—

but the code on it is set to change every four minutes. Just as Luna's malware is about to crack the code, it changes and the program has to start all over again. Whoever she's dealing with is a sophisticated programmer—not just an outcast in an old farmhouse, hacking into people's private CC accounts for rent money.

If she didn't know Margaret to be some evil mastermind who invented the stasis capsules and the brainwashing program, Luna would admire her. Never in a million years could she set up the kind of botnet Margaret Lewis has created.

"Any luck?"

Iris has sneaked in without Luna noticing. She wipes her forehead and reaches for one of the water bottles on the table. Instead of taking a sip, she presses it against her face.

"You need someone better than me. Someone more advanced. This woman is no joke."

"That's bad news for your friend downstairs."

Luna takes a deep breath, reluctant to take a puff of her inhaler in front of Iris. When in the same room with this woman, she'll stay strong—or at least seem strong—if it's the last thing she does.

"I'll try again. But all my rootkits and replay attacks have been blown. She encrypts everything. Even her AR-messages."

Iris walks over to the desk, pulls the drawer open. Without asking about the CS-key, she digs it out and places it on the table. The purple light does something to Luna's stomach. She's already drunk a few liters of water today, but she's able to keep it all down even though the light makes her gag.

"What about the computer the rebels use?" Iris' fingers tap the CS-key's screen. "As far as I know, this Kaarina chick is just a simpleminded runaway. What if we find a computer connected with Margaret's?"

"We'd need to know where to look." Luna pulls the laptop closer. "I'll check the deep web around Margaret's home address. If they connected the two devices before going their separate ways, Kaarina would have opened the laptop in the house before leaving."

Luna sets the bottle down, but her eyes refuse to focus. Instead of the desk, the bottle lands on the floor. Iris looks up from the CS-key. Her fingers stop their tapping and brush through her white and blue hair.

"You got those pills from the break room?"

"Why, you got a headache or something?"

It takes all Luna's willpower to raise her eyebrows and look innocent in front of Iris's amused look. Finally, the blue-and-white-haired monster puts the CS-key back into the drawer and fishes out a see-through package of what look like band-aids. She slides the box across the desk like a bartender sending a drink to her thirsty customer at the end of the bar. Luna catches it but doesn't pick it up to investigate it closer.

"Put one on. It's not blockers. Just a hint of morphine. It'll take the edge off."

Then Iris fishes out her AR-glasses and puts them on. Luna takes a band-aid out of the package. At this point, she'd be willing to eat a box of blockers and whatever brain-cell-damaging drugs this evil creature carries with her. But she sure as hell doesn't want Iris to know it.

Iris starts her AR-call. "Yeah. It's me. Anyone left on maintenance in the building? No, no guards. Just a driver. Mm."

The pain has now reached her neck and shoulders. Luna slaps the band-aid on. In two seconds, the stabbing sensation eases, turning into a slightly nagging throb. She fingers the inhaler in her pocket, wondering if she'll be able to wait until Iris leaves the room.

"Okay. Send him down and prepare a car."

Iris puts the glasses away. "Good news, Sleeping Beauty. One of the maintenance guys volunteered to take you home. Now, if only the numb-nut remembers to get a car from the Unchipped garage, you'll be home and sleeping in no time."

There's only one person in this building who would volunteer to help Luna. Other than Iris and Marić, only one person even knows that Luna exists. Annoyance flashes through her mind, but only for a second. The morphine spike wipes out all negative sensations. Soft, fuzzy, cuddling emotions are all she can feel in her numb and exhausted mind.

Steps echo in the corridor. A careful knock on the door. Iris walks past the man and leaves the room. Luna sits and stares at his kindly face. A friend. Or a foe? The band-aid stops her from caring.

"Ready to go, Bloody-Mary?"

A new car smell. Leather seats, cool and soft under her resting body. Dark woods, distant purple haze in the windows. The black Peugeot travels on the untended dirt roads, bouncing over potholes. But Luna doesn't mind the bumpy ride. She lies in the back seat, unarmed and unable to give a dog's turd whether her Chipped driver slaughters her in the woods or drives her safely home.

In the rearview mirror, Luna investigates Jovan's face—the little she can see of him.

His dark brown hair needs cutting. The curls hang down over his forehead, softening his sharp eyes. His straight nose and high forehead remind Luna of her father when he was younger. Handsome. Funny. Loving. But it's just a face, a surface. This man is not like her father. If anything, he's the reason why Luna's alone now. Without anyone to care for her.

Jovan hasn't said a word. It's like he knows how much Luna enjoys the peace and quiet Iris's magical band-aid brings her. It feels good not to care. To give in and let go. But the band-aid is losing its effect. Should she put another one on? Keep on riding this high?

She sits up in the backseat, takes out the package. Fingering one of the band-aids, she looks up at Jovan.

He meets Luna's gaze in the mirror.

"Quite a day, huh?"

What do you know about it? she thinks to herself.

"You could say that. Yeah."

"I didn't know you worked with Iris." Luna shrugs and doesn't reply. "She's really something, huh?"

Yeah. A real pain in my drugged ass.

"Not your usual every-day boss, I guess," she says.

Jovan laughs a bit, then sets his eyes on the road. It's getting dark. Driving on damaged roads is not the easiest task. Not without a self-driving car programmed to avoid potholes and craters in the road.

"Did you know she lived at the North Pole before?" Jovan says, drumming the steering wheel like they're playing tunes. But the car's radio is off. Nothing would come out, if they were to turn it on. Only static.

When Luna doesn't reply, Jovan continues. "Yeah, she worked with horses before. At some touristy place in an ice-hotel or an igloo. Something like that."

Suits Iris. Probably has an icicle where her heart should be.

"I'd love to go, one day," Jovan keeps chatting. "See the northern lights. If only to prove that they're not some ancient folk tale."

"Oh? Your Happiness-Program doesn't offer that? Northern lights?"

Jovan looks at her through the mirror. Their eyes lock for a second too long. Awkward and flushed, Luna looks away.

"Keep your eyes on the road. Wouldn't want to drive into one of the—"

The lurch and sudden stop send Luna flying against the front seat. Jovan's seatbelt stops him from flying over the steering wheel. The front of the car slips deep into a hole in the road. A creaking sound, and the tilted vehicle settles into its prison.

"Are you okay?" Jovan says and turns around, fighting with the airbag in front of him. The seatbelt digs deeper into his chest. It looks like it's about to split the man into two halves.

"I'm okay." Luna gets up from the floor, climbs back onto the back seat. She reaches for the door handle on her right, tries to open it. "It's stuck," she says. "Can we get out from the passenger side door?"

Jovan unbuckles his seatbelt. When it slides off his chest, he cries out in pain. His coveralls are ripped, showing a torn white T-shirt with blood on it. Grunting, he slides his body over and pushes the passenger door open. Then he extends his hand, gesturing for Luna to grab it. "Let me pull you up front first."

Luna takes his hand and crawls into the front seat. Jovan climbs out of the car and then helps Luna out. He takes a step back and investigates the car in the darkening night. "That's one big pothole right there," he says. "No way we'll get this thing out. Not if it's just the two of us."

"Don't the Chipped have a road service of any kind?"

"No need," Jovan says. "The self-driving cars don't drive into potholes. We'll see if they'll even bother coming to tow this thing back to the city. My guess is they'll leave it here to rot." One of the back tires is hovering above the cracked asphalt. Jovan kicks it, but the movement makes him wince in pain.

Why would she care if Jovan's in pain? Serves him right.

Luna fingers the band-aid package in her pocket. "Your chest. How bad is it?" she says.

"I'd need a light to see."

"You didn't bring your AR-glasses? What kind of a Chipped person are you anyway? I thought those things were attached to you by some kind of invisible magnet."

He reaches for his coverall's pocket and taps on it. "I've got them. But I know the light makes you sick."

Luna turns around and gazes at the night sky. "I won't look. Just take a peek." Out here, you can still see the stars. The farther away from the city's bright tiles and buildings, the less light pollution there is. But do the Chipped even care? Are they still interested enough in the real universe to look up at the night sky?

"It's not deep. But I better get this cleaned before it gets infected."

"You're calling them? To come get you?"

Jovan shakes his head no. "They won't come out here this late. I'll just walk back."

"It takes an hour to walk back to the city."

"Last I checked, I still have two legs." He waves Luna

off. "I'll be fine. How far from the farmhouse are we?"

Luna turns and points at the silhouette of a small hill and a tree fence in the distance. "If I whistled, the dogs would be here in thirty seconds. We're practically standing in the front yard."

"So you knew that pothole was there all along?"

Shit. Of course she knew. And it's not like her to forget something so important. But it's also unlike her to be this high.

Jovan waves his hand, a gesture for her to forget about it. "It's okay. You go home. I'll pick you up in the morning when there's daylight."

"Hey, wait."

Why? Why do you care? Just walk away. Go feed the dogs and hit the sack.

Luna walks over to him. She takes a band-aid out of the package and gestures for Jovan to move closer. She slaps the band-aid on his bicep. "For the pain."

"What is… oh." Jovan leans back against the trapped car, closes his eyes. "That's so much better. Thank you."

The AR-glasses blink in his hand. Luna looks away, but it's too late; the pain slams through her skull. It's as if she hit her head in the collision, but there's not a scratch on her body. Not on the outside of it anyway. She takes out another patch, slaps it on her wrist. Two seconds later, the wave of warm and fuzzy sensations washes over her body. She leans against the car, mirroring Jovan's relaxed posture.

They stare at the stars, smiling. Not talking.

Who cares if Jovan is Chipped? If he's a bad man? They all are. Luna's no better; she steals from innocent people. But that doesn't matter, either. Nothing does. Just the stars and the smooth waves of sensation moving through her body. Like she's a boat floating among the planets through neverending space. She lets go of her worries. Stops wondering when she'll be ambushed and turned into a machine. Whatever will be, will be.

A distant bark brings the star-gazing couple back into the moment. At least partly: They're both still riding the morphine waves.

"Your dogs?"

"Yeah. They must be hungry."

"How many do you have?"

"Oh, I've lost count. Thirteen? Fourteen?"

Jovan's smile turns into a grin. "I would love to see the one you saved in the woods that morning when we first met. Did she make it?"

Luna shrugs. She starts walking toward the farmhouse. "He. And yes, Buddy's still around. And in better shape than you are."

Jovan walks quickly after her, then slows his pace to match his footsteps with Luna's. They walk in the moonlight toward the old rotting Opel in the middle of the dog pit.

"And they won't attack me?"

Luna can't help but give him a smile. "One way to find out."

She didn't mean to invite him in. Or offer him half of Marić's leftovers in the fridge. Or clean his injuries and use most of the vet wrap and antibiotic ointment. She wanted to despise him, even after the second band-aid lost most of its effect. But still, here they lie, at opposite sides of her mattress, surrounded by a dozen dog snouts and twitching legs.

"What's this fella's name?" Jovan asks, scratching a black, curly-haired, dog head.

"I call him Mister Black."

His smile deepens as he cuddles with the half-asleep dog. "Hi, Mister Black. Nice to meet you. My name is Jovan, and I'm a friend of your human here… umm… well, this is embarrassing."

Luna rests her chin on Wacko's head. The mutt is sound asleep by her side. He was the only one who seemed skeptical of Jovan when they walked through the gate, though only for a second or two.

"You really don't know my name?"

"You never told me what it is. How would I know?"

"What did Iris call me? When she asked you to give me a ride home?"

"The Unchipped chick."

Luna huffs. "Go figure." She falls silent for a while. "I guess Marić is the only one left who knows my name. That I even exist," she mumbles.

"Marić's the one who runs the Chip-Charity program?"

"That's him."

"So let me get this straight," Jovan says. "You're not a big fan of the Chipped. Actually, you'd rather have nothing to do with us, or the city, or the Happiness-Program."

"Get to the point."

"So, you've decided that the Chipped are scum. But you're okay being friends with an Unchipped person who works for them? Who spies on people like you. Feeds them lies. Why is that?"

A strangling feeling rises in Luna's throat. Her fists clench. "It's not that simple," she says. "Marić's not a bad guy. We're all just doing what we have to." Luna wishes her voice didn't shake when she's angry. Who is this Chipped dickhead to judge Marić like that?

Jovan picks up the tension between them. He turns to lie on his back, staring at the ceiling where the Christmas tree lights throw their shadows. Buddy moves closer to him, snuggles against him. If these beasts were guard dogs, Luna would be the worst animal trainer on the planet. But she's not a trainer, or even a dog owner. She just provides homes to those who don't have one.

"How did you find these guys?" Jovan asks. The band-aid on his bicep must have worn off by now. But he seems to have melted into the mattress, enjoying the warmth and comfort of the creatures that surround him.

Luna hates to admit it, but she can feel it too. Peace. Quiet. Talking about the Chipped and Marić's job had interfered with it, but only momentarily.

She stares at Jovan's face in the dim light. Fighting it doesn't help—a smile spreads on her face. It's nice to have someone here. Even if it's a Chipped guy who might end up being the last thing she sees before she's stashed away.

"They're around. In the woods. By the harbor. Sometimes I feel like they find me and not the other way around."

Jovan turns to lie on his side. When he meets Luna's gaze, he smiles too. "How do you pick them?"

"What do you mean?"

"Well, there are so many strays out there. How do you decide which ones you bring home?"

Wacko starts snoring softly. Another dog climbs onto the mattress, rolls into a bundle between Jovan's and Luna's feet.

"I take in the ones that can't survive on their own. Most of the pets people set loose during the war have either learned to survive on their own, or they haven't made it. Some get stuck in the traps. Some get injured by another wild animal." She nods at the dog sleeping under Jovan's arm. "Buddy here stumbled across one of my security cameras in the woods. By the time it got dark, I was sure I wouldn't be able to find him. But you learn to track them down. And you learn to read them; who's aggressive, who's better off left alone."

"Do you let them out of the dog pen?"

"You mean, are they here of their own free will?"

"I guess that's what I'm asking. Yeah."

Luna supports her weight on her elbows and nods out the open sliding doors. "You see that raggedy-ass gate?" Jovan sits up, then nods. Luna lies back down and wraps her arm around Wacko. "Even Buddy could knock that thing down any time he wanted to. If they wanted to leave, they'd be gone. We're a pack now."

A comfortable silence falls between them. They listen to the dogs breathe, some of them snoring, some licking their paws clean and cuddling with their pack. Outside, the wind has started to blow. It howls through the Opel's windows, rattles the open glass doors. A chill travels through Luna's body. She looks around for a blanket but can't see one.

"Here…" Jovan pulls out a blanket that has fallen between the mattress and the wall. He spreads it on Luna's legs, then on his own. "I've forgotten what it's like to live without constant air conditioning, inside and out."

"Sucks, huh?"

When Jovan laughs, Buddy lifts his head and tilts it from side to side. "No, it's nice. Makes me feel sentimental. Like I've come back home."

She feels it too. Tranquility. *It's because you are home, dum-dum*, she thinks to herself. But she knows it's more than the waves of morphine, or even the fact that she's back with the dogs.

"Listen," he says, now dodging her gaze. "I'm sorry if I've been a bit too familiar with you. I guess I just wanted to, umm…"

Luna swallows loudly. She really wants him to finish that sentence. But at the same time, she wants to let him off the hook, because he looks more awkward and squirmy than she's ever seen him before. "Well. Thank you for saying that." She waves her hand. "Bygones now."

Jovan relaxes, a smile returning to his face. The comfortable silence settles over them.

"What do you do when you're here all alone?" he then asks. "How do you pass the time?"

Like a reflex, Luna's hand drops to look for the computer. It must be out of charge, but it's still stuffed into the broken mattress. She hasn't paid rent. Hasn't worked on hacking into Chip-Charity, or any other accounts, for days.

"See all these books around us?"

Jovan looks around and scans the towers of paperbacks, some scattered around the floor, some still rising tall in rows. "Yeah," he says. "They're kind of hard to miss."

"And you think they're just there for the dogs to chew on?"

Jovan reaches for a book on the windowsill. "It's been a while since I've held one."

"You don't read?"

"I used to," he says. "When I could still decide *what* to read." He flips the paperback around, then lowers it down to the Christmas tree lights so he can read the back. "His trade is murder. He's on the run…" he reads. "Horror?"

"Thrillers. And I know what you think."

"What's that?"

"That the last Unchipped living in the City of Serbia should read anything but. At least if she hasn't gone completely bonkers."

His laughter shakes the bed slightly. Luna can't help but chuckle with him.

"I don't think you're crazy. You're just a girl with many, many dogs. One that likes to read about murders and sleep with the doors wide open."

She opens her mouth to reply but changes her mind. Jovan's words caress her tired mind. It feels good to be seen. Even if it's through the enemy's eyes.

Pain. She jumps up and off the mattress, her mind still half-asleep. She hops around on one leg, holding her ankle with both hands. The bracelet from hell has come to life.

"Fuck, fuck, fuck!" she yells, jumping around the floor. The dogs circle around her, unsure of how to help. Jovan snaps out of his dream. Even though she's in excruciating agony, Luna notices how he's moved to the middle of the mattress during the night. Did they really sleep that close to one another?

Scratching his head, Jovan gets up from the bed. "What's going on?"

Luna grunts and keeps jumping, shoving Jovan aside. "I forgot to pay rent!" she yells.

"Rent? I don't understand."

"No, not rent! I'm late for work!"

"You're not making any sense," Jovan says. "What's wrong with your leg?"

Luna pulls up her pant sleeve. The tracker blinks and buzzes. The vibrating turns it around and around on Luna's ankle.

"Hold on..." Jovan says, patting his coveralls. Then he walks outside, pulls something out of the Opel's passenger seat. He's stored the Chipped technology in the rotting car, to spare Luna from its blinking agony. AR-glasses on, he steps around nervously, looking up to the sky.

Wacko barks once, nudging Luna's thigh.

"Food? Really?" Luna snaps at the dog. "You want to eat my leg too? Because I'm about to chop it right off."

Jovan talks to someone through the AR-glasses. Luna can't make out the words, but once he starts nodding, the bracelet simmers off. The pain is gone, but she feels dizzy. Like she's about to pass out.

Jovan walks back inside. "This is my fault," he says. "They never got my message about the car. Apparently, they thought we bounced."

"Bounced? As in fled the country? That's ridiculous!"

"Wouldn't be the first time. Thousands ran away to the United Inlands and City of Croatia during the war."

Luna sits down on the floor, rubs her ankle with

both hands. "No need to lecture me about the war. I'm well aware of the damage your people did."

He cocks his head. The AR-glasses now blinking in his chest pocket. "My people? What do you mean?"

"Are you slow or something? The Chipped. Your people. Capturing those who didn't want to live in some make-believe city, popping pills, and renting their brains for whatever clusterfuck goes on in those City-Centers." Luna hears herself, how pain and fear have made her mean.

Jovan shakes his head. "It's not like that. I know you think you know—"

"Oh, I know. I know you turn people into frozen potatoes in those hell-capsules. No need to deny it—I've been there. I was left to die in one. It's probably still down there, with my name on it."

Luna gets up from the floor, walks to the pantry closet. She rips the door open, and takes out two plastic scoops, lowers them into the dog chow bags. Jovan stands in the middle of the room, watching her gasping for air.

Jovan lowers his voice. "Nobody's dying in the capsules," he says. "In a way it's the opposite of that."

Luna throws the food on the floor. Instead of neat piles, the kibble spreads around the room, sending fifteen dogs scurrying after their breakfast. The clicking of nails against the hard floor is deafening. Luna is wheezing now.

Jovan hurries back to the mattress and brings over

the inhaler. Luna snatches it from his hand. "I don't need you to fetch me my things." She takes a puff. "You're not my dog." She walks outside, hoping the fresh air will ease her nerves. Jovan follows her, clearly not willing to let the topic go.

"Listen, I know what you're thinking. Trust me, I've been there myself. But you need to look at the bigger picture. Those people were going to die. Without the capsules, they would now be gone. They will be brought back one day. Once the program is more advanced."

Luna picks up a broken board from the ground, suddenly filled with rage and frustration. She swings the piece of wood against the Opel's side-mirror. The mirror takes off like a baseball, landing somewhere in the farmhouse's front yard.

"Tell that to my parents. They're sure as hell not coming back."

"What happened to your parents?"

"A riot." The wannabe baseball bat swings against a broken-down chicken coop. "The city." *Bang*. Against a flower bench, growing weeds. "The Chipped."

Jovan crosses his arms and leans on the sliding door frame. "I didn't know that," he says and then spreads his arms in defeat. "How was I to know?" He's about to say more but then sucks on his lower lip instead.

Luna throws her bat over the dog pen's fence. It clunks against a tree, lands with a dull thump. Not good enough. She needs to break things. Destroy. Revenge.

"You should know," she says, as she picks up one of

Marić's empty moonshine bottles off the ground. Her hand arcs back. "Because you spy on people." The bottle flies across the yard. It lands somewhere near the abandoned baseball bat. It doesn't break. "You stalk them. Follow them to their homes. Report them." Another bottle sails through the air, this time aimed at the main house's brick wall. This one shatters into pieces.

Jovan walks over. "I'm not a stalker. What makes you think that? The other day in the woods? That was just a coincidence, running into you there. I wasn't following you. Sorry for asking a few questions." He crosses his arms over his chest, frowning. "Yeah, I apologize. Silly me, thinking that maybe a girl covered in blood, chasing wild animals in the woods might need some help. Real foolish of me."

Luna lowers the third bottle she's about to throw. She turns around to face him. "A woman! Not a girl in the woods! A grown-ass woman! And I was doing just fine before you came along. Before you sold me out!"

He steps closer, raises his voice. "I did *not* sell you out."

"Words from the Chipped. Must be true."

"Why would I harm you?"

"Because you're all the same!"

"And you're too lost in your own little world to see that not all people are bad. Wake up, Bloody-Mary!"

"Don't call me that!"

They are standing so close now that he can feel her

breath on his flushed face.

"What else would I call you?" Jovan snatches the bottle from Luna's hand and throws it at the wall. "You won't even tell me your fucking name!"

Luna steps aside, picks up one empty bottle after another, chucking them at the brick wall. She screams, not words, just bottled-up rage and frustration. Fear too. She screams for what seems like forever until one of the bottles shatters Marić's kitchen window. Then she freezes, the next bottle in her hand and ready to go.

A faint whine reaches her ears. Out of breath, she peeks over her shoulder and sees a row of dog heads, staring at her, confused. Jovan bursts out laughing. Luna turns to glare at him, but can't help but join in his amusement. She tosses the last bottle. It breaks into thousands of pieces that land in a sizable pile of glass on the ground.

"Good aim," Jovan says. "That last one, I mean."

"Yeah, thanks."

"The second to last wasn't your best work."

The laughter bubbles up in her stomach, her chest. She's overwhelmed, nudged over some mental edge she didn't even know existed. Alone, but not really. Still alive but not for long. With a friend that might as well shoot her dead as soon as they get back into the city.

Once her breath evens out, and her outburst seems to have faded away, she side-eyes Jovan and gives him a nod. "It's Luna."

"Your name?"

"Who else's, you numb-nut?"

Jovan spreads his arms again, but his eyes are soft—full of warmth.

"Okay, Luna. What does a stalker need to do around here to get a cup of coffee?"

They arrive at the Chip-Center two hours late. Iris' blue highlights seem to glimmer in the sunlight, and the white locks of hair reflect the building's purple light. Jovan nudges Luna and leans in to whisper, "A vampire or a witch? Which one is your money on?"

Luna smiles but doesn't answer. She's not in a position to make fun of her current employer. Not the way Jovan is. Any day could be her last. Any minute Iris could decide that Luna's done her duties, ready to be plugged in and put away down under. They stop in front of Iris, wait for her to finish whatever she's watching through the AR-glasses on her head. Luna's fingers wrap around the last band-aid in her pocket. But it needs to be spared—she'll need it at the end of the day more than she needs it now.

Iris lifts her glasses and sets them on her forehead. She folds her arms and leans on the front wall, not looking either Jovan or Luna directly in the eye. The glasses are off, but she seems to still be somewhere else. Luna waits for her to say something like "You're late" or "No second warnings in the city. Down the stairs you go."

But she says nothing. Just stares over their shoulders. Jovan and Luna exchange a look. When the silence continues, Jovan shrugs. "I guess I'm off then." He waves briefly at Luna. "Thanks for the coffee, Bloody-Mary."

"Don't call me that," she says, but can't help the grin spreading across her face. Why does he have to be so easy to be around?

Jovan walks backward, beaming as well, then spins through the revolving door.

"She has three computers," Iris says, snapping Luna out of her reverie.

"What? Who?"

"She gave one of them to Kaarina. That's how they're connected."

"Margaret?"

"That's why they're always one step ahead of us."

Luna forces her thoughts away from Jovan to this moment in time and space. "But if it's Margaret's computer the rebels are using, it'll be secured just as well as everything else."

"No shit, Marilyn vos Savant."

"Who?"

"Just forget it. You need to connect with her outside the computer."

Luna tilts her head and stares at the creature in awe. "What, like a telephone call?" But she knows what Iris means. After unfolding her arms, Iris starts walking; but not through the revolving door. She drops the AR-glasses on the tiles. Then she peeks over her shoulder but doesn't slow down.

"You coming?" Iris says. "Or are you going to stand there playing dumb until doomsday arrives?"

Luna swallows, rubbing her sweaty hands together. If she follows Iris, no one will know where she is. Not that anyone in the city can be trusted—Iris would be Luna's last choice. But where is she going? What is she about to show Luna? How did she find out about Margaret's multiple computers?

"*O moj bože...*" she mumbles and jogs off to catch up with Iris.

Iris walks on the purple tiles, Luna right beside them on a slice of pavement. They're about to leave the AR-city behind and walk farther into what used to be farmland. Wanting to keep her mind clear for what's to come, Luna hasn't used the last band-aid in her pocket. Luckily for her, Iris has brought pain killers from the Chip-Center. Luna swallows them without any water, hoping they'll kick in soon.

Luna starts feeling better. Walking in the purple haze still sends daggers through her head, but the pills create a buffer, making the pain more nagging than stabbing.

Since they left the Chip-Center, Iris hasn't said a word. With her low but clear voice, she is singing a song in a language Luna doesn't know. But her voice is mesmerizing. How can something so evil hold something so beautiful within? Here they are, on a mission to capture people whose only crime is choosing their freedom. This creature wants them contained. In a glass box. Turned off and forgotten. In a way, that's worse than killing them.

Yet—it makes Iris sing. Luna doesn't want to listen, but the voice is like medicine to her aching ears. When was the last time she listened to music? Has she heard anyone sing since her mother died? Her mother always sang while cooking. While working in the garden.

The cityscape is left behind, and they move on into a lush field. Weeds and wildflowers decorate the overgrown path Iris now follows. The sun feels hot on Luna's skin. Thank goodness she forgot her hoodie back at the farmhouse. She wonders how Iris is so comfortable in her purple coveralls. They must have a built-in Thermo system or some other Chipped technology to cool her down.

The singing stops. Iris peeks over her shoulder, her AR-glasses covering her eyes. "You poor thing," she says. "Not getting to see this." Then she turns to continue down the path. Luna doesn't reply. She looks at the empty fields, watches Iris stop and stare at nothingness, a genuine smile on her usually apathetic face.

"This project was never finished, yet it's my favorite place in the City of Serbia."

"Project?" Luna asks, stopping at a reasonable distance from Iris' blinking glasses.

"The neon-forest, it's called," Iris says. She turns and points her finger at an empty space; at a patch of dead grass and hay. "A barn right there. Horses, ponies, and donkeys. I think they added a barn cat or two last year."

Luna twitches nervously. What is she supposed to make of this? Why is she here?

Iris continues walking and pointing her finger around the fields. "Mountains with snowy peaks. A real winter. Man, don't you just miss it? Skating and skiing?"

Sports? Really?

"I'm more of a walk-in-the-woods person myself," Luna mumbles.

"A tree hugger, then? I guess I'm not surprised."

The farther they walk, the thicker the wildflowers, weeds, and flora get. It feels like home—similar to the woods around the farmhouse that separate home from the old harbor.

Iris claps her hands enthusiastically and steps from the path. She continues toward the sun, her steps now bouncing with excitement. Luna follows her, admiring nature's rebellion. Thick stacks of centauries, holy brambles, and dog-roses bloom around them. It's hard to imagine that Iris's make-believe world can be more grounding for her than what's really out here. The peaceful silence, nothing but the wind howling in her ears. Luna's thoughts wander back to Jovan.

Iris stops and spreads her arms. A wide grin on her face, she seems to be hugging something invisible. Something enormous.

"We meet again," she says. "Reynisfjara."

The dry hay and grass rustles under Luna's hiking boot. Reynis-what? An AR-flower? A building complex?

Iris' laughter is like crystal. Like her singing, it soothes Luna's mind. She watches Iris spin around, her head tucked back, her AR-glasses pointed up toward the sky. A perfect row of white teeth makes her picturesque face glow with its own light—brighter and stronger than the blinking purple around her covered eyes.

Luna folds her arms and waits for Iris' dance to end. After a few minutes, her private party mellows down, and Iris sits on the ground to hug her legs. Her eyes are still gazing into space, her lips parted in a genuine smile.

Luna sits down too, a few feet away from the blinking purple. "Care to share with the class?"

Iris doesn't turn to look at Luna. She rocks back and forth, hugging her muscled arms around her legs. "They are pillars, just outside a tiny village called Vik," Iris says. "According to my people, the pillars used to be trolls, dragging a three-masted ship toward land. But the trolls took too long. In the morning, the first beams of sunlight turned them into stone."

Mythical fables? Iris may look like a fairytale, but Luna would have never suspected her of believing in anything but algorithms, code, and chemistry.

"Here near the cliffs... If you stand real close or sit still enough, you can hear the trolls moan and wail," Iris continues, her voice softer than usual. "They're homesick, longing for the mountains."

Could it be? She shouldn't ask. Shouldn't care.

"Are you homesick, Iris?" Luna wants to bite her tongue when she hears the empathy in her own voice.

Iris' smile fades away. She reaches for the AR-glasses, pulls them off. For a moment, the fragile expression on her face, her teary eyes make her look like a lost child. She brushes her fingers through the blue of her hair, looks over Luna's shoulder.

"Enough about me."

But they haven't talked about her at all. Not one word.

"Okay," Luna says. "Then tell me. Why are we here?"

Iris drops the glasses into her chest pocket. "I never believed in any of it. White magic. Black magic. Spells and shapeshifters. Not until I met your landlord."

Marić? What's the Reverend got to do with any of this?

"I used to think Marić had a hidden microphone. Installed under his skin or something phony like that."

Luna cocks her head. "A microphone?" Iris doesn't react to her, just keeps staring into space, talking to herself.

"And then we installed the AI cameras."

The Chip-Charity. Marić has collected CC's from communities and city citizens for years now. Controlling the faithful with religion. Controlling the faithless masses with fear. Fear of the grim fate that awaited those who abandoned their cities, those who ran off, got sick—or worse.

"It took us a long time to learn about the skill your kind has."

"You're talking about the tapping."

Iris smiles now and looks straight at Luna. "A power like that, to read people's minds..." She stops to shake her head. "It made me want to pull out my chip and become one of you."

This is news to Luna. She's always found tapping anything but desirable. Creepy. Nerve-wracking. Not once has she considered it to be a skill or an asset.

"But then..." Luna says, knowing she'd be better off not talking at all. "Then you wouldn't be able to hear the trolls."

A crooked smile on her face, Iris closes her eyes. "There are a lot of things I wouldn't be able to do. Such as making a difference. Changing the world. Curing the ill."

Are they still talking about fairy tales and alternate realities?

"But none of that will matter if they sabotage our work," Iris says. Her expression is back to its usual business-like, dull seriousness. Not a trace of magic remains. "Time to find that rebellious shit-mucker."

Kaarina. Iris wants Luna to tap her.

"That's not how it works, Iris."

"Works for Marić."

"That's different."

"How is it different? He thinks of a person, looks for them, they talk to him."

"True. But the people he connects with *want* to hear from him."

"Just try it," Iris says, shifting her weight. "You've seen her picture. You know where she is."

"If I knew where she was, I wouldn't be sitting here with you," Luna says. "I'd be home with my dogs. With Marić."

"Don't worry about Marić. He'll walk, I promise. Just humor me, Luna. Try it. If it doesn't work, we'll get back to the Chip-Center and create better malware. One that five Margarets couldn't stop."

She's never connected with anyone but Marić or Sloboda. Even those connections were short and rare—overwhelming. How is she to find a complete stranger? One that doesn't want to be found?

"Iris, the Unchipped are not the trusting kind. Can you imagine letting a complete stranger enter your mind? See through your eyes? Hear your thoughts?"

But Iris ignores her objections. She digs out the AR-glasses, turns her back on Luna, and dives back into the world of wailing trolls and charmed stone walls.

Sighing in frustration, Luna lies on her back to stare at the clouds sliding by. The wind has picked up again, but it's not chilly on her skin. No blankets needed in this weather. No Jovan's warm arm, resting against hers. The flashback from last night makes her stomach twitch. Had he meant to touch her?

She closes her eyes and thinks of the images on Iris' laptop. A man with dread locks. Another man, stern and big as a mountain. A younger looking fellow, with overgrown hair and gentle, friendly eyes. And then her, with a trail of scar—the mark of a knife—running over her cheek, down to her neck, onto her collarbone.

She turns her focus to the place she'd rather not visit. Deep within. One image after another flickers on her closed eyelids.

Her mother, singing into a wooden spatula.

Her father—his hands waving in the air as he gets to the climax of his nightly story by the fireplace.

Dirt-covered Wacko with a tennis ball. Shivering in the cool night. Abandoned and alone—just like Luna.

The images flash through her mind. One by one, she forces them away. Her mind keeps falling, searching, browsing. It's a free-fall into a state like the one she visits when she's fighting sleep. She knows she can't resist it or control it. And a part of her doesn't want to. The small piece of her that isn't too frightened to trust another human being.

Short blond hair, sticking up like a porcupine's quills.

Serene green eyes.

Unyielding stare. Pouting mouth.

"Margaret? Is that you?"

The voice inside her head startles Luna. Her eyes fly open. She sits up in a fraction of a second. Listening carefully, she holds her breath, doesn't reply. Another type of image appears; scenery. Circle-shaped windows. Mahogany shelves and cabinets, stuffed into a small space. Kaarina's surroundings sway back and forth, making Luna seasick.

"Ahh, wishful thinking," the voice continues. *"Do I know you? Are you in trouble?"*

Luna peeks at Iris, sitting a couple of feet away. If she has noticed Luna's sudden alertness, she doesn't let on.

"Is she holding you hostage? The girl with AR-glasses?"

Careful not to say a word out loud, Luna replies. *I work for her. Sort of.*

"How are you not in more pain? You're obviously not on blockers."

How do you know that?

"Because we wouldn't be talking if you were."

So that's what the blockers do. Stop Unchipped people from connecting with one another.

Pills during the day, morphine at night. It's only been a couple of days.

"I see."

They both fall silent, investigating each other's surroundings. But there's not much for Kaarina to see. Just endless fields and flora. Luna could be sitting anywhere. She suddenly understands why Iris picked this place.

"So you don't need any help?" Kaarina asks her.

Luna clears her throat but keeps talking silently. *No, I'm all set.* She tries to block the question from her mind. Tries to tell herself it's none of her business. And fails miserably. *And you? Do you need anything?*

"As a matter of fact..."

She looks around through Kaarina's eyes. The woman leaves the small, swaying room, walks out to a larger space with a full carpet. Slot machines rise around her, surrounded by dark-green velvet couches and chairs. It looks like a casino floating on water.

Kaarina keeps walking. She reaches a door with golden numbers by its frame.

495

She knocks on the door and enters. On the floor, a small child leans over a steaming bucket. A towel on the back of his head, he breathes the rising steam. When Kaarina enters the room, the kid looks up, his breath wheezing faintly. Kaarina sits down on the floor and replaces the towel, as the boy folds over the bucket.

"He needs an inhaler. Badly. I have three other kids with fevers, two of them vomiting and complaining of stomach aches. We need medicine. But I'm having a hard time connecting with any Unchipped people in our location. So far, you're the only one who has reached out. And I'm not sure where you are, exactly."

Luna holds her breath. This is all going wrong. She's not supposed to help them, she's supposed to capture them. And now Kaarina's offering her their location without her even asking.

Kaarina gets off the floor, walks out of the cabin. Back in the hallway, she turns to take a set of stairs that lead her up to a sunny deck.

A cruise ship.

How have the rebels got themselves a luxury boat?

Kids run around the deck, screaming and laughing. A smudged football exchanges hands as they chase each other around the empty pools and lounge chairs. A terrier—a Jack Russell—leaps into the air, trying to catch the ball even though it's the same size as his body. At the end of the boat, a row of people work around plastic tables and a fire pit that's tucked away from the playing kids.

Kaarina looks past the cooking adults. Docks, boats, roads, houses, abandoned vehicles, all abandoned and quiet by the shore. In the distance, a familiar-looking haze reflects faintly against the daylight.

"Please. If you could just point me in the direction—"

Luna cuts the connection. She gets up on her feet, paces in small circles.

She knows that harbor. That glow—the purple haze. She knows because she's in it.

Iris grabs her by the shoulders. "You found that sneaky barn rat, didn't you?" She shakes Luna, forcing her to meet her eyes. The AR-glasses are nowhere to be seen. "Where are they? Outside London?"

Luna blinks and tries to take a deep breath. When she reaches for her inhaler, Iris lets go of her. She pulls on her hair, pupils wide. "Well? Is Margaret with them?"

"I wouldn't know if she was."

"Where did they go? From Margaret's house? The old Wales? Former Scotland? Where's the English rebel hideout?"

"Beats me."

"But you were in her head. Saw through her eyes, for Vanir's sake!"

"Who's Vanir?"

"Just forget it."

Luna looks at Iris, making her breath even. She takes her time, giving her lungs time to take in the medicine she's inhaled. Then she shoves the inhaler back into her pocket.

"I wouldn't know where the base is in England. Because that's not where Kaarina is."

"They traveled? Again? *How*?" Iris brushes her hand through her thick hair. "Where? Where the fuck did they go?"

"They're right here," Luna says. "In the City of Serbia."

"Hey, wait up!"

Luna doesn't turn around. Jovan's footsteps echo in the Chip-Center's corridor. She carries the laptop and the CS-key to an empty lobby desk and sets them down. One last task for Iris and she'll be free to go. Why she couldn't just leave the equipment in the office, Luna has no idea. And she doesn't care. The only thing in her mind is the fact that Marić's already biking home to the farmhouse, or so she's been told.

A hand stops her before she steps into the revolving door. "Hey, Luna. Hold on," Jovan says. "You're leaving early today. Did you get in more trouble for being late?"

Luna shakes her head. "It's not me who's in trouble." Images of kids playing with a small terrier flash through her mind. Has she made a mistake? Telling Iris where Kaarina is? "But now that you mention it, I did get fired. In a manner of speaking."

"Iris let you go? You don't work here anymore?"

She shrugs a shoulder. "Free as a bird," Luna says. "Now, if you'll excuse me, I've got dog mouths to feed."

Jovan follows her outside. "Hey, can I see you later? Tonight? There's something I really need to tell you."

But Luna's too stuck in her own mind. Thinking of a kid, folded in half over a steaming bucket. Thinking of Iris, gathering her soldiers to make a special trip to the Old Port of Belgrade. In the basement, hundreds of stasis capsules wait for those whom Luna has betrayed.

"Luna? Hello?"

At least she didn't mention anything about a cruise ship. Just the harbor. A general direction. That would buy Kaarina and her rebel crew some time. Before they're turned into fish food.

A hand shakes her shoulder. "Hey? What's gotten into you?"

She steps away from Jovan. "Take your Chipped hands off of me."

"What's wrong with you?"

"With *me*?" she scoffs. She feels like crying but doesn't want to do it in front of Jovan. Or anyone in this rotting, evil city. "There's nothing wrong with me. I'm great, actually. Swell. Instead of the basement, I'm heading back home. To hang out with my dogs. Eat some chocolate and read some books. See, Iris is sparing me for now. They're done slicing into my brain and playing with my mind. Turns out, I'm worth something. Not just some insignificant Unchipped person, desperately holding onto her so-called life."

"Everyone's worth something," Jovan says, staring at her with wide eyes. "Not a single human being is not worth saving."

"You mean storing? In a capsule? Unconscious?"

Jovan lifts his index finger to his lips. "Not here. If you just meet me tonight—"

"I'm done listening to your Chipsplaining! Go away, Jovan. Go back to whatever you do to help these brain-scavenging, god-complex-driven maniacs."

She turns to walk away. *Please follow me. Please come after me*, she thinks, but no footsteps light the tiles next to her.

Jovan has gone back inside. Back to a reality where trolls and fairies are as real as blind people seeing and the deaf hearing. He's walked away from Luna.

She may be free—but she's also more alone than ever before.

The barking reaches her ears as soon as she gets to the first camera—hidden by the dirt road that leads to the farmhouse. It's not just Wacko. It's all of them. Fifteen sets of paws drum against the driveway.

Luna breaks into a run.

Glowing red, the flames greet her as she passes the security camera. Somewhere inside the burning farmhouse, her laptop is beeping out of control. She can hear the beeping from here. How is it still working? Luna looks around the premises and sees a pile of cardboard and wooden boxes—filled with her belongings. The Christmas tree lights hang on the side of a box that used to serve as her nightstand. A corner of her laptop peeks out from the box.

"Marić?" she calls out. His bike leans against one of the trees at the opposite side of the yard. A single duffel bag rests next to it, a picture frame poking out of its side-pocket.

"Marić, where are you?"

The dogs gather around Luna, looking up, barking. When Buddy starts jumping against her thigh, Luna kneels down and pets his head. Wacko's head appears immediately, licking the side of her face. "It's okay, guys." She looks up toward the flames. "Just please tell me he's not—"

"What, you think I'm suicidal now?" Marić's voice startles her. "Just because the Chipped have no use for me?"

Luna spins around and stares at the reverend, who has come up behind her holding a half-empty bottle of moonshine. He takes a sip and says, "I guess that's not far from the truth. Now that I think about it."

"What the hell happened?" she says, now standing up. With a few long strides, she reaches Marić and pulls the bottle from his hand. "Did you even try and put it out?"

"What, the fire?"

"Yes, the fucking fire," Luna says. "What's wrong with you?"

From the back pocket of his work coveralls, Marić pulls out another glass bottle. He pops the cork, takes a sip. "Now, why would I put out a fire that I started?"

Luna looks at the burning house. The yard and the dog pen. The sliding doors are open, the edge of her mattress engulfed in flames. The Opel's silhouette is barely visible through the blaze.

"She wouldn't approve of this," Luna says. Marić takes another sip. He doesn't need to ask who Luna's talking about. "I know she made you promise to take care of me."

"And how would you know that?" Marić's words have started to slur. He's been at it for some time.

"I know because she made me promise the same thing."

"Hm." Another sip.

"And now you've made us both homeless."

The reverend sits down on the gravel and sets the bottle aside. Arms cupping his knees, he watches the flames pierce the roof. "This is me, taking care of you," he says. "It's time to let go of this place. Get back to the real world."

Luna scoffs and spreads her hands. "This is the real world. Not that neon-crap they feed you in the city." Her head twitches back. "Of course," she says, laughing a little. "They *made* you do this. Forced you to decide for both of us. Let me guess, I'm now their newest programmer with a hefty salary and a luxury apartment. And what about you? What did they give you in exchange? A fucking mansion?"

"They didn't make me do shit."

"Oh yeah? Then why would you do this?" Her hand gestures at the burning house. "Why give up on the last piece of freedom we've got left?"

"You call it freedom. I call it being a prisoner of the circumstances." Marić gets up, takes another sip of moonshine. "Look around, Lu. This place, this reality. It died long ago. We're all that's left. You and me."

"You sold me out."

"I did no such thing. You can still do whatever you want, Lu." Marić picks up the duffel bag, throws it over his shoulder. "I know I am."

"I thought you said they let you go? That the Chipped have no more use for you?"

"I did. And they don't."

"Then where the hell is your drunk ass pedaling to?"

Marić smiles at her. He places the open bottle into a basket attached to the bike's handlebar. Sloboda used to collect flowers in it when biking around the countryside. The pollen of each new bouquet had made Luna sneeze for days.

"Don't worry about it, Kiddo," he kicks the bike forward and jumps on. Wobbling on the gravel, he looks back over his shoulder and yells, "I have a date with the only freedom I care about."

Long after Marić's bobbing bike disappears around the tree line, Luna stands and stares at the road. Tiny's high-pitched whine mixes with the crackling sound of the flames eating away her haven.

Luna picks up Tiny, caresses her heart-shaped head, kisses her chubby cheek.

"What did he mean, Tiny? Where is he going?"

Just a bike and a duffel bag. He had left everything else behind.

And also a picture frame.

A picture of Sloboda.

"Sloboda…" Luna then mumbles. "Of course."

In her native language, the name stands for the thing we all crave.

Freedom.

The room sways smoothly around her. Luna digs deeper into the blankets. All she needs is right here, in a cruiser boat she and the dogs have snuck into: blankets, curtains, dishes, carpets. While all the stores, offices, and houses have been stripped clean, the outcasts seem to have forgotten about the harbor and its boats. She now understands why Kaarina and the rest of the rebels have decided to hide in the cruise ship not too far away.

A clank in the small kitchen corner snaps Luna awake from the edge of sleep. Wacko's paw digs out pots, plastic containers, toilet paper—and a bag of oyster crackers. The yellow mutt picks up the bag of unexpected treats and walks to Luna. In front of the bunkbed, he cocks his head, the bag hanging from the side of his snout.

"Go crazy, my friend," Luna says. "Have at it."

Wagging his tail, the dog rips the bag open. Crackers fly out, causing a ruckus as fifteen dogs go after them with gusto. But Luna barely notices. She closes her eyes again, restless thoughts filling her tired mind.

Marić, joining Sloboda. In other words, choosing to die. For the first time ever, he hasn't answered Luna's attempts to tap him.

A rebel leader, hiding in a cruiser with sick, innocent kids. About to be ambushed and taken away.

Jovan, in the Chip-Center, wondering why he ever bothered to talk to a low-life like Luna in the first place.

The boat sways in the wind, but the nausea it causes is nothing compared to the last days spent in the AR-city. On the nightstand next to Luna lies a box of her things. She reaches for the Christmas tree lights, pulls them out of the box. After folding them into a messy bundle, Luna presses them against her chest and pulls the blanket over her head.

Maybe the Chipped will find her too. The soldiers won't know how to tell her from a rebel—she'll be hauled away just like they will. Iris would know, but why would she care? Everyone's replaceable.

"Serves me right..." she mumbles. One of the dogs jumps on the bed, wrinkling an empty plastic bag. More clinking echoes from the kitchen corner. More hidden treasures are being pulled out. More snouts at work trying to feed themselves.

Luna thinks of Iris, stuck in a job that gives her meaning. It makes her think she's saving the world instead of slaughtering it. How Iris once enjoyed things like mountains, the ocean, old barns, and equine companions. Things she loved so much that she has arranged a fake reality just like the one she used to live in. What stops her from going back? Did her old home burn down too?

She thinks of Marić, tortured by the memory of the kind, loving Sloboda. How he dedicated his life to giving people hope and faith—no matter what the motivation behind it was, or if he believed in it himself. Luna once heard him late at night, talking to Unchipped people around the world. Some stuck in the middle of a plague. Some searching for a church to pray in one last time.

Jovan. He says he didn't report Luna after bumping into her in the woods. She doesn't want to believe him. Doesn't want to be deceived again by those who have turned against her kind. But in her gut, she knows Jovan told her the truth. It wasn't him, snooping around the farmhouse, collecting pieces of rope and moving the brick that kept the doors shut. He was there only once—invited. Sleeping in her bed, sharing a moment of hope and peace in the middle of the chaos.

The world has come to an end. The cities are humanity's last, desperate attempt to keep its shit together. But just as it always does, history will repeat itself. People will go after what they believe to be the one and only truth.

Like Marić biking into the city for his assisted suicide.

The pressure at the back of her head grows stronger. She fishes out a fresh package of band-aids in her pocket; a last gift from Iris. Fingering the box, Luna wonders how long it'll take for these headaches to stop for good. She'll never go back into the city. Never again will she stare into blinking purple lights or CS-keys that hurt her body and mind.

The pressure becomes more demanding. Just as she's about to slap the morphine band-aid on her arm, Luna recognizes the reason behind her slight headache. It's not just a ghost pain or an aftershock of what she went through earlier.

It's someone tapping her.

"Marić? Marić, listen to me. Don't—"

"It's not him, Luna. It's me. Kaarina. Please don't block the connection."

She sits up on the bed, surprised. Why is Kaarina still able to contact her now? Why haven't Iris's soldiers captured her already? Luna had considered talking to her—warning her—but never in a million years did she think there was still time to do that. Kaarina should already be a goner. And so should everyone else she's with. Though late, Iris' soldiers will arrive in the harbor any minute now. She should tell them they're coming. Tell them what she's done. But it's useless now. It would only cause panic and chaos.

"I know you're in the City of Serbia. I saw your Chipped friend's purple AR-glasses when we last spoke. Listen, I really do need your help. The kid you saw, Ricky, he really needs that inhaler."

Luna fingers the inhaler in her hoodie pocket. Without the reverend, she will soon run out of medicine herself. And without a fresh inhaler, her lungs will burn and be destroyed, just like the hundreds of paperbacks lost in the fire.

"Please, Luna. The reverend told me you'd help me. He's the only one who has answered my tapping."

"It's because there's no one else left here to tap. It's just me and him. And the two of us aren't talking right now."

"Where are the rest? The Unchipped and Chipless?"

In a basement. Plugged into a capsule. You'll see it for yourself soon.

"The Inlands. City of Croatia. Doesn't matter. They're gone," she says. "Aren't you afraid I'll tell the Chipped where you are?"

"The reverend said you would never do that."

Luna's stomach flips. Nausea washes over her.

Kaarina paces around a slot machine, rubbing her

shaking hands together. *"Is there an old pharmacy anywhere nearby? A store that might still have supplies left? Please, Luna. I'm begging you. He'll end up dead."*

The laptop in the cardboard box starts beeping. The daylight through the boat's window is enough to charge its solar battery. The beeping is for the malware, installed in the Chip-Charity accounts, indicating progress. But Luna ignores it. There's no more rent to be paid. No need to steal more CC's from anybody. She just needs to find enough food to survive.

Three of the dogs appear by the bed. Luna forms a silent question with her lips; *What?* Three tails wag from side to side as they stretch down on their front paws, ready to play. Wacko brings over a plastic container, nudges it toward Luna and the bed.

What will the dogs do when Luna's gone? How will they survive? With no food, no skills to hunt down anything but bags of oyster crackers and an occasional dead mouse.

At least their injuries have healed. They're all healthy. They aren't fighting for their lives. When she looks at them more closely, she can see the happiness and joy shine in their playful eyes. They're not suffering. Not like those in Kaarina's care.

But it's not her problem. Why should she care? She won't. Doesn't. It's too late. But if she could at least give her the inhaler... maybe that would count for something. Luna buries her head in her arms and exhales.

"Get up to the deck," Luna says. "Look for an old church by the ferry ticket office."

Kaarina takes off running. She climbs the stairs, bangs the door open, and steps into daylight. Through her eyes, Luna watches the sun set on the quiet harbor.

"A bit more to your right."

Kaarina's eyes finally lock on the church. *"I see it."*

"Across the road, the second boat docked by the water jet. Blue and white stripes. See it?"

Kaarina looks for the boat, finds it. "Yes, it's right there."

"Good. Come get your damn inhaler. I'll trade it for some of your Jack Russell's kibble."

CHAPTER 5
THE BASEMENT

A knock above the cabin reaches Luna's ears. It ends the dogs' wild playtime with emptied closets and a couch pillow jumping course. Two of them have turned random pieces of clothing and rags into weapons for a tug-of-war. The pressure at the back of Luna's head returns.

"That's enough," she tells the barking dogs. They sit on the floor, Wacko grunting disapprovingly.

"Can't you just knock and tell me it's you?" Luna yells under the blanket. "You know, like a normal person?"

For a moment, it's quiet. Then a muffled chuckle. The sharp bark of a terrier.

"See? Your dog gets it."

The hatch opens. Kaarina's face peers in, eyes searching for Luna. The dogs go wild again. The Jack Russel above starts barking. Only Wacko barks back.

"Ässä, hush," Kaarina hisses. Then she looks at

Luna. "Should we come down? Or do you need us to keep our distance?"

Luna sits up on the bed. "Why? You carrying a taser gun or a deadly virus?"

Kaarina smiles but stays above the stairs. "Most of us have a hard time trusting each other. And I can't really blame anyone for that."

"Right. Because we're all just a bunch of nut-cases. For damaged people like us, every sharp object is an opportunity."

Kaarina tilts her head. Her terrier does as well. "What?"

"Nothing. Forget it. Just cabin fever." Luna crosses her legs on the bed and reaches for the inhaler in her pocket. "Tell you what. See that yellow goof?" Luna nods at Wacko. "If you can climb down those stairs without him showing his teeth, I'll make you a cup of tea. Plenty of gas left in that stove, if you can believe that."

Kaarina hesitates for a few seconds, then drops her legs down the hatch. She looks at the pacing Jack Russell. "Ässä. Stay." The dog steps toward her and puts its paw on Kaarina's face as she starts climbing down the stairs. "No. You stay. Little shit," she mumbles.

"Not into training them, huh?" Luna says, keeping her eyes on Wacko. The mutt sits by the stairs, staring at the approaching stranger.

"He's my mother's dog," Kaarina says, making her way down the steps. "We were both raised never to do anything just because someone said to."

That night at the farmhouse, Wacko hadn't let Iris anywhere near the pack. With Jovan, the mutt had allowed him to walk right through the broken gate. When it comes to people, Luna trusts this dog's intuition more than her own.

Kaarina stops on the last rung of the ladder, looks at Wacko. "Okay if I jump down, friend?" A tilt of a head. Then—a lazy wag of a tail. Kaarina jumps down the ladder and kneels to scratch Wacko behind his ear. "Thanks, Bud." A wet tongue travels across her face. The terrier starts barking fiercely above them, but Kaarina ignores him, laughing and scratching. "Don't listen to him, Bud. He's always bitching. Full of made up problems, that terrier."

Luna gets up from the bed and walks over. The boy wouldn't have time for many puffs; Iris' soldiers must be approaching the harbor as they speak.

"Here," she says, handing over the device. "I hope your kid feels better soon." If Luna's to have an asthma attack, she's as good as dead. But better her than the kid.

Kaarina takes the inhaler and shoves it in her pocket. "Not my kid. But we take care of each other, nonetheless. Margaret would kill me if I let that boy die."

Luna perks up when she hears the familiar name. "Margaret Lewis? The programmer?"

"Of many things. But yes."

"You do know that she's one of the people who

created the Happiness-Program, right?"

Kaarina smiles. "I guess I have friends in high places." She takes off the black backpack she's carrying. From inside, she pulls out three see-through plastic bags of dog food. "I thought I brought you plenty. But it looks like it won't last you more than a day or two." Once the dogs see the kibble, they surround Kaarina, all sitting down patiently, waiting to be fed.

"I was only joking about the dog chow. But thank you." Luna turns and heads back to the nest she's made of blankets and sheets. "Do me a favor and open one for them. Just sprinkle it around on the floor. They have their dog-politics all worked out. No one's ear is going to get bitten off."

Still smiling, Kaarina does as she's told. She opens the bag and leaves small piles of dog food around the cabin floor. Each time a dog comes over, taking its turn to eat, she scratches its face or neck. "The kids would love these guys. They adore Ässä, but if he doesn't see a ball he can chase after, he couldn't care less."

Good news, Ässä, Luna thinks. *Soon there'll be no more kids around to pull your tail.*

Kaarina looks up in wonder. "What do you mean?"

Did I say that out loud? I'm sure I didn't.

"No, you didn't," Kaarina says. "But the connection is open. I can read your mind, remember?"

Fuck.

The last couple of days—Iris, the CS-key and hacking, the purple city, their hike into the make-believe reality—it all flickers through her mind. And Luna lets it. It's too late anyway. And if this Unchipped leader strangles her for betraying her own kind, so be it. She'd rather Kaarina do it than the Chipped in the city.

Kaarina sits down on the cabin floor. She rubs her temples, shaking her head. "They're onto us? Why hasn't Margaret warned us?"

"Because we're onto—" It's Luna's turn to shake her head. "*They're* onto Margaret. Iris found out she's helping you."

"How?"

"Iris hacked into an old security camera next to Margaret's place of residence. Caught you and a bunch of dudes coming in and going out."

Kaarina reaches for the backpack on the floor. She pulls out a laptop, opens the screen. "You got access to the Chip-net?"

"That's what you use? The Chip-net? How is that thing so hard to break into?"

Kaarina's fingers move quickly over the keyboard. "It's all cryptated."

"You mean encrypted."

"That's what I just said," Kaarina mumbles. She types in a message, hits enter. A whooshing sound tells them the note has been sent. She closes the laptop and shoves it back into the bag. "And I thought this would be the last place they'd catch us."

Tiny makes her way over, starts licking the visitor's face.

"Why did you come here in the first place?" Luna asks. "Why City of Serbia, of all places?"

"Bill didn't have much money left. It took months for the community in the City of California to gather enough CC's for us to fly out of England. But once it was time to go, there weren't just twenty-something of us traveling. It was a hundred and something seats we needed in that airplane."

"The kids?"

"Loads of them. Margaret could only take Hannah and Noah to the city. They were about to have a baby. But the rest of them had to flee."

"And why hasn't Margaret joined you?"

"I have no idea."

"And Serbia was the cheapest flight to take?"

"It was practically free. No one travels here because of the war. But the Chipped still order imported goods from the other cities. We traveled with bags and boxes filled with black tea, potatoes, cereal, and wine. The black-market people told us the city abandoned the harbor. That we'd be safe here. And I guess they were right."

"Until I came along," Luna says, her voice breaking.

Kaarina looks up to investigate Luna's face. "You think I blame you?"

A short laugh escapes Luna's dry lips. "Why wouldn't you? I worked with them. Led them right to you."

"Yes, but you did it to save your friend, the reverend.

They blackmailed you, Luna. I can't blame you for what you did."

Luna clears her throat, but all words fail her. How is this person not angry? Why is she still here, talking to her, when the enemy must be halfway down from the city?

"Shouldn't you warn them? The kids and your friends?"

"I've already tapped Yeti. He's on the lookout."

"Yeti? Is that a Finnish name?"

"It's the abominable snowman." Kaarina waves her off. "A long story. We're better off staying in the cruise ship. If we leave the harbor we'll get caught by the cameras."

Luna nods, staring at Kaarina's backpack. "Can you move the cruise ship?"

"We'd need a local CS-key to move the boat. And medicine to make it across the ocean."

"And go where?"

Kaarina reaches for the backpack, pulls out a memory stick. "It's a map. And a weapon of some sort, to defend ourselves. That's what we picked up from Margaret's house that day."

"Defend yourselves from what? The Chipped?"

The short curls around Kaarina's face dance slightly as she shakes her head. "That's the thing; I don't know. She said that one day those I trust the most will turn against me. And that's when I should open the file. But it won't open. It's also cryptated, and none of us know how to break the code."

"Why won't Margaret open it for you?"

"She said she'd help when it's time. That I shouldn't open it until all hope is lost."

"A Chipped army marching to get you isn't a hopeless situation in your books?"

Kaarina nods. "I've just sent her a message." She points at a watch on her wrist, the kind that people used to integrate with their computers. "But she's not responding. Which has never happened before."

They exchange a look of terror. Luna says it first. "Iris. They got her."

Kaarina throws the memory stick across the room. She screams like she's in sudden pain. Luna swallows painfully. This is all her fault. She did this.

"That's it," Kaarina sobs. "We're doomed."

Buddy takes off after the object their visitor has thrown across the room. His tail wagging, he fetches the stick and brings it to Luna. She takes it from the dog, stares at its scratched plastic cover. Then she storms to her computer and pushes the memory stick into its designated slot.

Kaarina paces in circles. Her low mumbling tells Luna she's in the middle of a conversation with one of her people. Maybe with that boogeyman. What's with the fairy tales lately?

Luna shakes her head to try to focus. Green numbers and letters blink in front of her. She has to make this right. Fix this. Whatever it takes. Multiple windows pop up on the screen. Luna types in codes and they disappear. She keeps trying to break the code, but all her attempts fail. She's too focused on the work to notice Wacko next to her—Kaarina's tiny laptop in his mouth.

"Wacko, that's stealing. Put it back…" A wide grin spreads across Luna's face. "Bud, you're a genius!"

She takes Kaarina's computer, opens it up. She types in one command after another, learning Margaret's encrypted programs—her way of thinking. In just a few seconds, she knows how to get into the Chip-Charity accounts. She could empty them now if she wanted to. But stealing money is not a priority right now. Over a hundred lives depend on Luna's programming skills.

After five minutes of research, she returns to her own computer with the memory stick installed. Her fingers fly over the keyboard. She enters a new search, then another code. After five attempts, the screen fills with a green checkmark.

She's in.

"Kaarina? Tell the snowman you've got to hang up."

Kaarina rushes over and leans in to see the screen. "How the hell did you do that?"

Luna doesn't reply. She flicks over the file. Only two documents; a map with coordinates and a snippet of code.

"Is that a map of…" Kaarina starts.

"Yup," Luna says, her fingers still moving rapidly on the screen. "Looks like she's sending you to Iceland."

The cruise ship smells like cigarettes and oatmeal. A guy called Micky rushes to shake Luna's hand. "Thank you for helping us," he says, not letting go of her hand.

"No need to thank me," Luna says, smiling. "I'm the reason you're in this mess."

He waves her off, but the frown on his face reveals the white lie. "Not to worry. We've been through worse."

Kaarina is talking to a man the size of a mountain. Luna doesn't need to ask to know who it is she's talking to. A young girl, maybe seventeen or eighteen years old, brings Luna a cup of steaming hot coffee. Her name is Ava. She's holding onto a smartphone like it's glued to her hand. "Drink it while it's hot," she says.

"Thanks, Ava."

Yeti walks over to Luna and nods at her. A friendly face follows his lead; a familiar face, one that Luna's seen many times on a laptop screen in the city. Markus. A Chipped rebel from the City of Finland.

"You said there are no guards in the lobby?" Yeti asks her. "That the revolving door doesn't lock?"

Luna shrugs. "Who would they try to keep out? There are no rebels left to break in. They're about to chase and hunt us down. No way they'd ever think we would just walk into the Chip-Center willingly. It's the last place they'll look."

"How about surveillance cameras?"

"There are a few, sure. But there are no break-ins. Not in the Chip-Center, or anywhere in the city.

Whoever is checking the buildings once a day and then calling it a day."

"And the unused CS-keys? Downstairs in the basement?"

Luna nods. "With tons of medicine. If they haven't moved it all, that is. But I don't see why they would."

He nods approvingly. A barking sound startles him, making him jump. "Bill? Can you take those dogs somewhere else, please? So we can get going?"

The guy with the dreadlocks laughs happily as he wrestles with two of Luna's dogs. He ignores Yeti and his request.

Shaking his head, Yeti refocuses on their crew of four. "All set?" Yeti asks, holding a rifle and a tranquilizer gun.

"Ready when Luna is," says Kaarina. Her smile is a mixture of stubbornness and nervousness.

Luna pets Wacko's head, then leans over to kiss him. "Don't let them get you, Wacko. Not without giving them hell."

Just as Luna thought, the lobby of the Chip-Center is empty. Purple light shines through the revolving door. The city is quiet. A row of self-driving cars stand parked by the center's outer wall; Iris must have led her soldiers into the harbor on foot.

Luna waves her hand, gesturing for Yeti, Kaarina, and Markus to follow her. She slides into the revolving door, surprised by the force of her sudden headache; it knocks her off her feet.

Shouldn't she be used to this by now?

It's Markus who picks her up by the armpits and pulls her up straight. "Kaarina and Yeti are struggling too," Markus says. "How did you survive working here?"

Luna pats her pockets, then remembers that she handed all the band-aids to a Spanish-speaking woman downstairs by the cabins. The woman carried a rifle on her back and refused to tell Luna her name. But she gave the medicine to her anyway; the sick children need it more than Luna ever will. It won't last them long, though. Neither will Ricky's inhaler. They need more medicine for everyone to survive the long trip they're about to take. They need buckets full.

"In the break room, there's a medicine box," Luna says to Markus. "You should get it open. The light won't bother you." She leads Markus to the break room with Yeti and Kaarina following right behind, holding their heads in agony.

This pain she's experiencing is more than the headache. Luna's painfully aware of the challenge of her personal quest in the center: finding Marić. She needs to at least try and talk some sense into him. Try and get him to come with them. The reverend isn't answering her tapping. He seems to be out of reach. First Luna panicked, thinking he was dead. But then Ava reminded her of how the blockers work; how the substance in an

Unchipped body would stop them from connecting with others of their own kind.

He wouldn't have killed himself. No—he must be in the Chip-Center. And Luna would do her best to find him before fleeing the City of Serbia for good.

In the break room, Markus pops open the purple glowing medical box. He rummages through the packages and pill bottles, then opens a container and takes out familiar-looking pills. Luna takes the pills from him and passes the bottle to Kaarina. "They're not blockers. Just painkillers. You'll still be able to talk to Bill."

Kaarina hesitates, her hand hovering above Luna's open palm. "You're sure? You've taken these before?"

"Trust me. Your head's going to explode and pop right off if you don't."

Giving Luna a half-smile, Kaarina nods and takes the pills. Luna does the same. Yeti reaches for the bottle, pours half of its contents into his mouth. Teeth crunching the pills, he walks over to the medical box and shoves what's inside into his pockets. Then he nods at the corridor, "Lead the way, Lu."

The nickname he uses brings Luna's thoughts back to Marić. Once again, she taps for him, but the connection remains blocked. She starts to walk down the corridor. At the end of the hallway, she opens the basement door and walks down the stairs. Her friends follow her, closing the door behind them.

"And you're sure this is where they store the

medicine?" Kaarina whispers.

"Yes. There's a space with shelves and drawers, filled with what I believe to be their belongings. Stored away for later."

"*Their* belongings?" Markus says. He points a flashlight at Luna's face, blinding her.

Yeti snatches the flashlight from him, points it at the closest row of stasis capsules. "You're saying you haven't seen them before, mop-head? Go take a quick peek in." The light reflects off the tinted glass, showing something solid inside. Markus walks over to the light beam. Pressing his forehead against the glass, he looks into the capsule.

"Oh, my god!" he cries suddenly, stumbling backward. "How many?"

Yeti doesn't reply. His flashlight flickers between the capsule rows, gesturing for Luna to take the lead. She starts walking down the path she once ran through, heading the opposite direction.

They walk in silence. Markus gasps for air as he passes the endless glass prisons, all holding a living human being inside. Kaarina and Yeti follow in Luna's footsteps, staring straight forward, ignoring the blurred, empty faces around them.

"Once you see them through the tinted glass, you can't unsee them," Kaarina says with a low voice. "You shouldn't have made him look in."

"He gets on my nerves," Yeti hisses back at Kaarina. "He's like that fucking dog of yours. Always panting, constantly snooping."

"Better than humping anything and everything that moves."

Yeti's low laugh rumbles in the open space. "Jealous much?"

Luna gives them a look. They fall silent, the robust man fast-walking to reach Luna's side. "You think your friend is down here? The reverend?"

"I do. I don't know where else he would be."

"Do you know where exactly? Where would they keep someone about to get plugged in?"

"There are stations for patients. Operating tables. I know, because I woke up on one."

"They chipped you here?"

"They put me into a medically-induced coma. I was never supposed to be here for this. I only had trouble breathing, a lung issue. Nothing to do with my brain."

Yeti's teeth grind. He seems to be pondering whether to keep talking or not. He peeks over his shoulder, checking the distance between them and Kaarina and Markus. Then he leans closer to Luna to whisper. "They did the same to me. Chipped me against my will, at least in a way. I was going through a rough patch back when... You know what, doesn't matter. These people are fucked up. Big time. I'll do everything I can to find your friend."

The flashlight's beam reflects against something not made of glass. The supply station is still there, just like Luna remembered. She takes off running, Yeti following her closely. Once they're over by the storage area, Luna starts pulling the drawers open.

"Here, grab a bag," she says, tossing the fabric bags around the floor. "The medicine is in the drawers. I'll grab the CS-keys. Oh, and if you see any inhalers, I could use one or two of those."

Kaarina kneels next to her with an open bag in her hands. She starts tossing in packages and pill bottles, without reading their sides or checking their labels. "Leave the water bottles," she says. "Plenty of that on the boat."

Markus takes out four sets of purple coveralls and checks the sizes. "Here, put these on. Just in case we bump into guards or soldiers on our way out."

They stop filling the bags and put the coveralls on. Yeti's pant legs end just below his knees. The zipper won't shut over his broad chest. "Oh for fuck's sake…" he mumbles, leaving the zipper be. He reaches his arm toward one of the shelves and swipes a row of band-aids, gauze, and medical wrap straight into a purple bag. Then he walks to Luna, grabs her by the arm.

"Is the operating station far from here?"

She shakes her head for no.

"Alright. Kaarina, we're going to take a tour around this lovely little chamber. We'll be back by the time you run out of bags to fill."

Marić's silhouette on the table is the first thing Luna sees. She runs straight toward him, with Yeti's heels thumping against the tiles right behind her. As soon as she reaches him, she starts shaking the reverend's lifeless body on the operating table. The chipping helmet rests next to him on a metal tray.

"Marić, wake up!"

Yeti picks up an electric pad by the helmet. He taps the screen on, reads the text out loud.

"Unchipped: Dragan Marić.

Fifty-four-year old Chip-Charity Director.

Re-chipped attempt February 2089. Operation failed.

To be stored in stasis 79132. Next to wife Sloboda Marić, stasis 79131. City of Serbia."

Luna stops shaking the Reverend, turns to look at Yeti. "What did you just say?"

"It's just basic info with the capsule location."

"No, no. About Sloboda. His wife."

Yeti looks at the pad again. "She's in capsule 79131."

Luna grabs the flashlight from him and starts running down the rows of pods. She reads the numbers on their side, keeps running. With Yeti's shouts in her ears, she looks for the capsule that contains Sloboda–a person she thought was buried in the backyard back at the farmhouse. Why is Sloboda here? She can't be. She's dead. Isn't she?

The capsule she looks for appears in a row so far away from Marić, Luna's not sure she'll be able to find her way back. But she can't focus on that right now. She needs to find Sloboda, save her if she can. After all the woman's done for Luna, she owes her that. And a lot more.

"Seven-nine-one-three-one," she says, repeating the number over and over. "Seven-nine-one-three—"

Just like the rest of them, the capsule hums on a tile base. Luna steps closer, presses her forehead against the tinted glass.

A chest with freckles.

A face, closed eyes.

Full lips, parted slightly.

It's her. Only her thick, red hair is missing.

The footsteps reach the capsule. Yeti, out of breath, circles around the capsule, looking for its pad. "There are instructions," he says breathlessly. "On how to open the helmet she wears. It'll unplug her from the capsule, but I don't know what else it'll do."

"Can't we just pull the capsule plug?" Luna asks, her voice raspy and panicking.

Yeti pulls out a pad from a slot behind the capsule. "The capsule gets its electricity from the tiles, and the tiles run on solar electricity. I don't know how to operate the power system they've got going. There are no instructions for that. Just the helmet."

Luna circles the capsule, running her hand around its smooth surface. "There's no handle or knob. No buttons. How do I open this thing?"

Yeti swipes and scrolls on the pad, reading the screen. "Here," he says. "It says to push the door in with two hands. It should then slide open."

Luna pushes the front of the capsule. A glass door sinks into the capsule, then smoothly opens. Sloboda looks like she's sleeping, with a blinking helmet on her shaved head. Other than the headwear, she's naked.

Yeti steps closer, reaches for the helmet. Luna steps in to block his way. "I don't like you seeing her naked like this. She was a very private person."

Surprise lingering on his face, Yeti stares at Luna in the dim light. "You're serious?"

"Dead serious."

"I don't think this is the time and place for subtlety," he says, but turns his back anyway. "Fine. You do it."

Luna leans into the capsule and reaches for the helmet. "There's no switch. Do I press on it, the same way as the door?"

"No, it's different. There should be three buttons on each side of the helmet. You need to press all six buttons at the same time, press and hold, until you hear a whooshing sound."

"That's what it says? *Whooshing* sound?"

"Just push the damn buttons, would you?"

Luna fingers the side of the helmet, her face so close to Sloboda she can see the faint hair above her upper lip. She finds the buttons, closes her eyes, and presses them all at once. Three seconds, nothing happens.

"It's not working."

"Keep pressing."

Ten seconds pass. Fifteen. Twenty.

"I'm telling you, it's not working."

"You have to give it some time. It's a hard shutdown."

Twenty-eight. Twenty-nine. Thirty…

Whoosh. The helmet opens on its hidden metal hinges. Carefully, Luna pulls it off Sloboda's head. She fixes the short hair on the side of her face. Waits for her to wake up.

"Is she breathing?" Yeti asks, without turning around.

"Yes, she's breathing," Luna says. "Now take off your coveralls and help me put them on her."

"You want me to blindfold myself first?" Yeti says, but starts stripping off his overly small purple attire. Luna waits for him to make an inappropriate comment on her request for him to strip. But he never does. He brings over the coveralls, then helps Luna pull the unconscious woman out of her prison. He holds her limp body up while Luna wiggles the pant sleeves on, then pulls the rest of the coveralls on. Once the zipper is closed, she nods at Yeti.

"Let's get her the fuck out of this hell-hole."

When they get back to the operating table, Kaarina and Markus hover over Marić, supporting his upper body while the confused reverend rubs his head. Yeti leans over to Luna and whispers to her, "I don't think it's a good idea for him to see his wife like this. I'm going to go around the capsule rows. Take her back to the stairs."

"Wait, you're leaving us?"

"No, I'm not leaving. But I don't care how full of piss and vinegar you and Kaarina are, I don't see you dragging anyone who's unconscious out of here. And don't get me started on the mop-head. He's clumsy as fuck."

Luna nods, and Yeti disappears behind the humming capsules. She hurries to Marić, reaches for his hand. Markus lifts up a package, much like the morphine band-aids Luna's familiar with.

"We gave him something to wake him up," Markus says.

Luna nods and turns to Marić. "What the hell happened? Did they knock you out cold?"

Marić looks confused, staring into Luna's eyes but not seeing a thing. Then his head shakes from side to side. "They prepared me. I should be with her."

"Yeah, about her. I thought Sloboda died. That we buried her behind the farmhouse. You and me. Just like she wanted. I dug the freaking grave myself."

"You did. And then you left."

"So you never buried her. And now she's suddenly stored away like a potato in a cellar? Living and breathing?"

Marić buries his head into his hands. "I couldn't let her go, Lu," he says. "I had to bring her in, ask them to save her for later. Doctor Solomon told me she's this close," he shows a gap with his thumb and index finger, "to curing Glioblastoma. Maybe she'll make it after all."

"That's insane, Marić. It was her time to go. She *wanted* to go."

"And now it's mine."

Kaarina and Markus exchange a look. Luna walks over, leans in to hear what they have to say.

"It's his decision, Luna," Kaarina says. "Maybe not with his wife's life, but he can do whatever he wants with his own."

Should she tell them about Yeti, carrying Sloboda to safety? It wasn't up to Marić to stop Sloboda from dying. But is it really Luna's right to bring her back to life?

She walks back to Marić. "We found a way out. There's another option. We can leave tonight."

"I can't leave her here," Marić says.

"What if we were to bring her with us?"

"She would die. Maybe in a few days."

Luna squeezes Marić's hand, looking deep into his eyes. "Marić, she wanted to die. She'd never agree to be trapped in a capsule in some basement."

Slowly, he pushes one leg over the table, then the other. By the time he stands up, supported by three petite people, Yeti runs over to them, carrying six purple bags, bursting at their seams. "Ready to go?"

Marić looks up, measuring Yeti from head to toe. "Lu? Where did you find a giant and a pair of minions?"

Luna rolls her eyes at him and smiles. Together they start toward the basement stairs. "I don't know, Marić," Luna says. "Sometimes, I feel like they're the ones who found me. Not the other way around."

Yeti hands over the supply bags. The door opens above the stairs just as he is about to pick Sloboda up. They scatter, retreating behind the stasis capsules. Yeti stands with his back pressed against the base of the staircase, hiding in the shadows.

Steady, smooth steps light the staircase tiles, one at a time. The blue in her hair changes into a deep shade of purple as Iris steps down, looking around in the dim light.

"I get it, Luna," she yells. "I really do. What's more important than helping those in need?"

Iris stops at the base of the stairs, only a few feet away from Yeti and Sloboda. Her hand hovers near her belt. Luna can't see the dart-gun, but she knows it's there. Iris's cat-like steps take her further into the basement. She peeks behind one stasis capsule, then another. "You think we don't have cameras down here, you silly girl?"

Call me a girl one more time... Luna thinks, clenching her fists. Kaarina's voice immediately echoes in her mind. *"Don't let her provoke you. Stay put."*

Iris moves deeper into the basement. Yeti's voice booms in Luna's head, followed by Kaarina's words.

"I need a distraction. To get up the stairs with the body."

"Don't call her that. She's not dead."

"For the love of..."

Luna doesn't understand Yeti's foreign words, but she's pretty sure he's cursing. After counting to ten, he continues to argue with Kaarina inside Luna's head.

"Okay. I need to carry the lady *up the stairs. You need to distract the* lady *that carries the gun. Better?"*

"Distract her, how?"

"I don't fucking know! Throw something."

"I'm not wasting anything in these bags on that lunatic."

"Kaarina, I swear—"

That's when Marić steps into the light. He was hidden behind one of the capsules, separated from the rest of them, surely listening to their telepathic conversation. Has he seen Sloboda by the stairs?

Palms facing forward, Marić gestures for Iris to lower her gun. "It's just me. Put the gun down."

Iris aims the dart gun at Marić. "Where are they?"

Marić lowers his hands. "Gone. They left through the second staircase at the other side of the basement." Marić takes one step back, then another. "You're too late." He keeps backing away from Iris and the gun, luring her further and further away from the stairs.

"Go now," Kaarina says inside Luna's head. Yeti appears from the shadows. He moves noiselessly to the base of the stairs. Luna holds her breath, watching him and Sloboda make their way up, one silent step at a time.

On the last step, he needs to adjust Sloboda's weight on his shoulder. The purple coveralls rustle faintly. Luna's eyes flicker to Iris's back. Has she heard the sound? Yeti freezes in place. If Iris turns around and sees him, her dart will be far too fast for him to escape.

Marić, talk to her, Luna says, tapping her ex landlord. But the connection is not there. She speaks to him anyway. *Don't look at the stairs. Keep your eyes on Iris.*

Marić clears his throat. "You got anything to drink around here? My throat is killing me."

Iris cocks her head and lowers her gun. "You expect me to believe that you woke up from forty milligrams of Thihexamine. On your own. To find a nightcap?"

"I know. Crazy, right?" Marić walks over to a random stasis capsule and knocks on its glass. "How do these things work, anyway?" He pushes the front with two hands. "Can I open one and see?"

Iris hurries over to him, deeper into the basement. "Stop that," she says, her gun still pointing at the backing away reverend. "Are you still high? Or drunk? Suits you better."

Yeti's boot touches the last stair. Then the doorway. He disappears into the purple haze above the basement.

"What can I say," Marić says, "I like my moonshine."

A movement at the opposite side of the capsule rows catches Luna's attention. Kaarina and Markus move slowly toward the staircase. *"You next, Luna,"* Kaarina says silently.

Not without him, she thinks, staring after Marić and Iris, now deep down the dark basement.

"I made my choice, Kiddo," Maric suddenly says. *"I may have not honored Sloboda's wish to die. But I'm not going to betray her again. I promised to take care of you."*

And I promised her to keep your stubborn ass alive. I'm not leaving you.

"Please, Lu. Let me do this. Just go. Leave me. That's my *last wish to you."*

All Luna can do is swallow her tears.

Kaarina continues. "*Now, Luna. Go. Get to the stairs. Watch your steps. You have to keep going, and whatever you do, don't look back.*"

Marić's words echo in the basement, but Luna can't hear what lie he's decided to tell Iris next. Taking short but determined steps, Luna gets to the base of the staircase. Iris's silhouette has moved further away. But if she turns around, she'll have no trouble taking Luna down.

Marić and Iris take turns speaking while Luna makes her way up, one step at a time. Left foot, right foot, left, right. At the top of the stairs, she sidesteps and presses her back against the wall. Yeti gestures for her to join him. He's kneeling down behind an enormous Yucca palm tree, but the plant is hardly enough to hide his wide frame.

A loud bang echoes from the staircase. The dart-gun goes off in the basement. Luna turns to run back in, but Kaarina and Markus block her way. The basement door closes behind them and they make a break for the revolving door.

"Go, go, go," Yeti says, pushing Luna onward. She runs with them toward the exit.

What happened, Kaarina? Is Marić okay?

But Kaarina doesn't answer—silently or out loud. She just keeps running.

Marić? Marić are you okay?

But the connection is no longer there. It's blocked and gone—just like the man who has now fulfilled his promise to his dying wife.

They run through the narrow alleyways, dodging cameras when they see them and keeping an eye on any movement in the city streets. Yeti takes breaks to adjust Sloboda's weight on his broad shoulder. They're moving slower than Luna wishes they would. She can see the frustration on Kaarina's face.

After their fifth micro-break, Kaarina walks to Yeti and leans in to hiss at him. "You need to keep up with us. They're checking the cameras as we speak. It's just a matter of minutes before they find us."

Yeti cocks his head, staring at Kaarina. "Oh, we're in a hurry? Why didn't you just say so? I thought we were sightseeing—"

"Quit being a wise-ass and move."

"I'll stop as soon as you quit being such a di—"

The self-driving car appears out of nowhere, blocking them into the alleyway. Yeti lowers Sloboda down on the ground. Then he clenches his fists—ready to fight.

The car door opens. A man with purple coveralls jumps out of the vehicle but freezes by the door. He raises his hands in the air, waving them at the approaching Yeti.

"Hold on, man. I'm here to help."

Luna takes off running. She wedges herself in to block Yeti's way, pushing his chest to stop him. "No, no, no. Don't hurt him. He's with me!" she yells, banging her fists against Yeti's steel-hard body. "It's my friend, Jovan. He won't hurt us!"

Yeti stops, staring at Luna in awe. "You're friends with this Chipped scum?"

"He's not scum. And he won't report us. He... he wouldn't. He's just here..." But Luna doesn't know how to finish that sentence.

Jovan takes a step closer, turns Luna to face him. Before she can do a thing, Jovan presses his lips against Luna's. Yeti scoffs at the kiss and spreads his hands in a huge shrug, but Luna only partly notices. Images of Christmas tree lights blink through her mind. She closes her eyes and pretends they're back at the farmhouse. Surrounded by fifteen dogs. Tucked away from the world gone wrong.

When Jovan pulls away, he presses something in between Luna's palms. "So you can reach me," he whispers.

Luna tries to look at the object in her hands, but Jovan shoves it into her pocket. "Not now."

"When?" She places her hand on the object inside her pocket. "And why are you giving me a set of AR-glasses?"

"So you can reach me."

Luna stares at the glasses in her hands. Then she shakes her head, her eyes drilling into Jovan's. "Come with me. Why would you stay here?"

"I can't. Not just yet. I'm needed here."

"To do what?"

"I'll tell you all about it, one day. But for now, the glasses will connect us and keep you safe when everything else falls apart. And it will, Luna. It'll all collapse one day."

"What do you mean? When is that going to happen?"

"You'll know when. Just remember, nothing is what it seems. Trust your gut. Forget labels," Jovan says and then turns to face Yeti. "The soldiers are looking for you everywhere, but I know a road they're not tracking. Here," he hands a note to Yeti, "It'll take you there safely."

Kaarina steps forward. "And the soldiers in the harbor? What happened with the cruise ship?"

"Everyone's still there," Jovan says. "I checked it personally."

"What do you mean, checked?" Markus asks.

"We were told to check all the boats in the harbor for fugitives. I checked the cruise ship near the church." Jovan stops and smiles at Luna. "Looked pretty damn empty to this soldier."

"A soldier?" Luna stares at him in disbelief. "But you don't wear..."

Jovan grabs Luna by the shoulders. "Yes, a soldier. Undercover and Chipped. Like I said, there's a lot I need to explain to you."

The others start heading toward the road Yeti's leading them to. Luna hugs Jovan, squeezing his purple coveralls into her closed fists. Jovan hugs her back and says, "You trust me?"

Luna nods, burying her face in Jovan's chest. "But should I trust them?" She looks up and nods at Yeti, Kaarina, and Markus. They've stopped running, to wait for Luna.

Jovan cups her face between his hands. "There's no them. Or us." He kisses Luna again and then wipes the tears from her face. "Just people. Winging it. Doing what they can in a world where it's impossible to know what's best for them."

EPILOGUE
OPEN SEA

The cruise ship glides forward on the tranquil open sea. The laptop placed between her legs on the sunchair, Luna stares at the flickering green numbers. One window after another opens, showing snippets of code and green checkmarks. Luna fingers the memory stick, making sure it's installed correctly. After being carried between Wacko's teeth, Kaarina's laptop case is full of dents and scratches.

But it works perfectly.

A *bling* sound tells Luna the CC's from yet another Chip-Charity account have been successfully transferred to an account William gave her access to. Bill also told Luna about Hawk, a rebel leader who runs a community for Chipless people somewhere near the City of California. He didn't tell Luna where. Just smiled and mumbled something about being willing to kill for a fish taco. Hawk is connected with the black-market and transferring funds through her accounts, so that Bill's

money will stay untraceable.

For what seems like the hundredth time since they escaped through the Old Port of Belgrade, Luna taps her hoodie pocket, making sure it's still there; a set of AR-glasses. Jovan's gift to her. No purple light blinks on these glasses. No other colors, either. They're made for an Unchipped to use—for Luna to connect with Jovan. A man who saw to the heart of her and made her trust other human beings again.

Wacko barks once. Ässä joins in, his bark relentless and unceasing. The terrier circles the yellow mutt, rolling onto Wacko's back and then up again. Wacko makes his way over to Luna, licks her thigh, and nudges her hand. The same hand that's wrapped around the glasses inside her hoodie pocket.

"What? You finally find a friend who is just as obnoxious as you are. And you're going to leave him high and dry?"

Kaarina laughs and turns in her lounge chair. Her pale skin is turning red around her V-neck T-shirt, and the tip of her nose is peeling. "Ässä's shenanigans get old pretty damn fast. Can't really blame Wacko."

"Like owner, like dog," Yeti says. He dodges the sunscreen bottle Kaarina throws at him.

The girl with the smartphone—Ava—approaches, carrying Buddy in her arms. She sets the dog down on the deck, then tucks the phone into her back pocket. "Ricky is up on his feet again."

"Great," Micky answers, clapping his hands

together. "And the fever patients?"

"Asking for more crisp-bread and root beer."

Markus laughs happily. "We're doomed. The kids are eating all our grub."

Kaarina sits up in her chair and nods at Luna. "Once this mastermind has finished cleaning out the Chip-Charity accounts, the black-market can deliver us more food than we can eat."

Bill comes over, sits next to Luna. Playfully, he nudges her in the ribs. "How did you pull that off anyway? I thought Margaret was a wizard when it comes to this stuff. And *poof*—you just break into a system she created?"

Luna blushes and turns her face away. She's not used to people complimenting her. Telling her "good job." Not since Sloboda's fake death. She now rests in one of the cabins downstairs, breathing steadily but not coming out of her unconscious state. What if Sloboda never wakes up? And even if she does—will the tumor in her head put her down again?

"I'm afraid I can't take much credit," Luna says to Bill. "It was Margaret's code that got us through the system. In a way, she hacked her own system. I was merely a middleman."

"Speaking of," Bill says. "Where the hell is she? Margaret?"

Kaarina frowns. She peers at Ava before she replies. "I'm not sure. I don't think she'd be able to escape City of England. Not without a rebel community to help her hide or escape. And as far as I know, the red city has none of us left."

The images of people exchanging goods in a security camera feed rushes back into Luna's mind. "That's not completely true," she says. "I've seen people over the cameras. In the city, but helping those outside."

"Back in England?" Bill says, his voice filled with surprise. "Are you sure?"

Luna nods. "Maybe your friend is involved with them."

Ava looks up. "If they're helping people to survive, Margaret will be involved. That's what she does. Helps those who can't help themselves."

Wacko's bark interrupts the silence that follows Ava's words. Luna smiles at him, grateful to have her dogs and this unexpected new family around her. But somehow their company also reminds her of those who are not here—and how much she misses them.

She wants to call Jovan. Lock herself in a cabin. Turn the AR-glasses on. Hear his voice. But any device connected to the Chip-net might give the Chipped new hints about their whereabouts. Kaarina's laptop is the only secure device; running code and relieving the leaders of the Happiness-Program of their CC's. But the AR-glasses, she's not sure of.

"What if they track us down?" she says, turning to Kaarina.

"I thought you destroyed the boat's tracking system?" Yeti says. "I thought we're offline?"

Unsure what to say, Luna shrugs. "I did. We are."

Her fingers find Jovan's glasses in her pocket. "I guess I'm just paranoid."

Kaarina turns to Markus. "Does anyone here have more information about the Chipped technology? How the headquarters keep tabs on its people?"

"I can ask," Markus says. "But if they're having this much trouble finding us, I'm pretty confident they don't have any ultimate tracking devices out there."

"Mop-head's right," Yeti says. "But nonetheless. I do suggest we shut off all devices that are not encrypted or approved by this nerd here." Yeti nods at Luna. "At least until we get to Iceland."

Kaarina's frown deepens. "He's right. Any cellphones—"

"Hold on there, Kay. Did you just tell me I'm right about something?"

"Well, you *are* wrong too."

"Oh, good. For a moment there I thought you were running a fever."

Kaarina waves Yeti off and turns to face Luna. "We should keep all technology shut down. Just like chuckle-nuts here said. Especially when we get to Iceland. This is a new start for us, but most likely also the last one we get. One phone call or encrypted connection gone wrong, and it could all be lost again."

"So... what?" Bill asks. "Toss them over?"

They all fall silent, holding onto their devices, staring at the open sea.

Luna clears her throat to talk. "Just turn them off.

For now, that's good enough. We'll figure out more after we dock."

Ava shoves her smartphone back into the pocket of her jeans.

Kaarina nods at the second laptop in front of Luna. Luna reaches for its lid, shuts it down.

The light on Bill's CS-key turns dull gray.

Luna fingers the AR-glasses—a secret inside her hoodie pocket. A secret between her and the one she failed to save.

Turning away from the others, she turns her focus within. She can't use the glasses to call Jovan, so she taps for Marić instead, knowing there will be no response.

But she speaks to him anyway.

Hey, friend. How's life as fish food treating you? I just wanted to say... thank you. For carrying me home that day. For letting me steal your coffee and chocolate. Which reminds me, I still owe you last month's rent.

Wacko jumps on Luna's chair and presses his body against hers. The dog senses more than his goofiness would suggest. He knows that even though Luna is surrounded by her new pack, she mourns the ones she had to leave behind. Blinking her eyes to hide her tears, she wraps her arm around her best friend.

So I guess this is goodbye, you grumpy old fart. I'll save you some moonshine until we meet again. Luna hides her tears in the dog's long yellow fur. *Thank you for taking in a stubborn underdog who didn't understand that all this time—she's the one who needed to be saved.*

Shoot! Book 4 of the Unchipped story is at a close. But don't worry, you can find out what happens next in Book 5 in the Unchipped series, UNCHIPPED: The Resort available on Amazon

My dearest reader,

You are simply amazing! Thank you so much for your support and readership! I can't tell you how much you reading this book means to me. I'm humbled and honored that you've dedicated your valuable time to experience the Unchipped universe with me. I'm still a newbie author, so if you were to leave me a review on Amazon it would be a huge help! Short or long, doesn't matter. Reviews are the best way to help other readers find the Unchipped Series.

Want to stay in touch? I would love it if you'd subscribe to my newsletter @ www.TayaDeVere.com/HappinessProgram Starting in August 2020, newsletter subscribers will receive free, exclusive early access to in-universe short stories from the Unchipped series a week before each book comes out. That's every eighteen days so be sure to sign up to get first crack at the series!

Facebook – facebook.com/tayadevereauthor
Instagram – instagram.com/tayadevere_author
Goodreads – goodreads.com/tayadevere

Bookbub – bookbub.com/authors/taya-devere
Amazon – amazon.com/Taya-DeVere/e/B07KRJPMTV

Gratefully yours,
Taya DeVere

THE END

About the Author

Taya is a Finnish-American author, writing contemporary fiction and dystopian sci-fi. After living and traveling in America for seven years, she now lives in Finland with her husband Chris, their dog Seamus, three bunny-boys (Ronin, Baby, Loki), and her horse of a lifetime, Arabella.

Best things in life: friends & family, memories made, and mistakes to learn from. Taya also loves licorice ice cream, secondhand clothes and things, bunny sneezes, salmiakki, and sauna.

Dislikes: clowns, the Muppets, Moomin trolls, dolls (especially porcelain dolls), human size mascots and celery.

Taya's writing is inspired by the works of authors like Margaret Atwood, Peter Heller, Hugh Howey, and C.M. Martens.

Final Thanks

Anyone who's ever spent more than five minutes with me knows that animals hold a special place in my heart. Ever since I left Finland and moved to England to work with horses in the summer of 2009 (has it really been over ten years?!), horses, dogs, cats, bunnies, and other critters have become the center of my world. I've seen terrible things and wonderful things, lucky animals and not so lucky animals. I've done my best to help as many beings as I can, but without a doubt, I've received more love and comfort from the animals in my life than I've been able to return. It will take a lifetime to balance the scales

And I'm not alone. I've met so many fabulous people who really care about animals, from the pets we consider family and who share our homes, to the animals that we admire from afar in the wild. These beautiful minds tend to go the extra mile when it comes to loving our four-legged friends. We all do this in our own ways, and I firmly believe that there's no right or wrong way—not when you mean well and always remain kind.

So I want to say THANK YOU to all who have dedicated any part of their lives to helping and loving animals. I know so many of you but will list a few that immediately pop into my mind:

Thank you, Luna Mrkovacki, Teri Crutchfield, Jackie Blackwell, Ann Seamonds, Jack Phoenix, Eila Ahokas, Chris DeVere, Andrea Ward, Cara Mancini, Chris Ryan, Sybille Crafts, Janette Ruonti, Outi Törmänen, Jessica Freiman, Leila McCarter, Martha Scheffer, Sari Holmström, Shelly Harkins, Tara Vaughan, Zoë Flannery, and Zoë Waterson. This world is a kinder place because of you.

The Unchipped series – Release schedule 2020

UNCHIPPED: KAARINA - 8/31/2020
UNCHIPPED: WILLIAM - 9/18/2020
UNCHIPPED: ENYD - 10/6/2020
UNCHIPPED: LUNA - 10/24/2020
UNCHIPPED: THE RESORT - 11/11/2020
UNCHIPPED: LAURA - 11/30/2020
UNCHIPPED: DENNIS - 12/18/2020

CPSIA information can be obtained
at www.ICGtesting.com
Printed in the USA
LVHW030922111020
668496LV00001B/196

9 789527 404126